'Tell Uncle David all about it.'

A soft giggle escaped her. Uncle David! She'd never had an uncle like Dr Kent. Juliet sighed. 'I don't really think I can tell you. It's so private, you see.'

There was a pause. He seemed to be scrutinising her, and she felt her colour rise.

'Tell me, Juliet, would you hesitate to tell your own doctor this problem that's worrying you to death? Can't you trust me enough to keep it between just the two of us?'

She looked into his brown eyes. They were watching her intently, with a look that disconcerted her and excited her at the same time.

Dear Reader

Variety is the spice of life and that is certainly true of Caroline Anderson's book this month, set in a busy accident and emergency department. A strong book medically, and emotionally. We also have a cruise setting, a hospital librarian heroine from the Norfolk coast, and a student nurse with a real problem to solve that could affect many lives. Four books to get your teeth into — enjoy!

The Editor

Alice Grey really intended to be an artist! She did nurse training instead, followed by midwifery and health visiting while her two sons were small. She has been writing since the age of fourteen, but Medical Romances are a change of direction for her, and she wishes she had begun writing them sooner. She lives on the borders of Birmingham and Worcestershire, with her husband and two cats.

Recent titles by the same author:

THE DOCTOR'S VISITOR
TANSY'S CHILDREN
THE BABY DOCTORS

HEARTS IN HIDING

BY
ALICE GREY

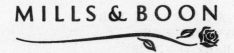

MILLS & BOON LIMITED
ETON HOUSE, 18–24 PARADISE ROAD
RICHMOND, SURREY, TW9 1SR

First published in Great Britain 1993
by Mills & Boon Limited

© Alice Grey 1993

Australian copyright 1993
Philippine copyright 1993
This edition 1993

ISBN 0 263 78347 2

Set in 10 on 10 pt Linotron Baskerville
03-9310-63737

Typeset in Great Britain by Centracet, Cambridge
Made and printed in Great Britain

CHAPTER ONE

'YOU'RE going back already? You've only just arrived.' Penny Rogers leaned back in her chair and surveyed her colleague with mildly amused eyes.

Juliet Avery adjusted the belt around her slim waist. 'I have a ward visit to make. Sister said I could.'

'Well, if Sister's sanctioned it, it can't be to Melrose, where that dishy registrar's often to be seen.'

'I work on Melrose. Which doctor's that?'

'Kent, of course — David Kent. You must have seen him! He's single too, from what I've heard.'

'Penny, you're the limit! Why should I be interested in the private lives of the doctors? We're not all —— '

'Then you're the only one who isn't. Oh, of course — I forgot. You're going around with that ex-fractured tib and pelvis, aren't you? The wealthy one whose father owns a publishing firm. The filthy rich.'

Juliet couldn't stop the slight flush that stained her pale cheeks. 'That wasn't the reason I went out with him,' she said defensively. 'Nigel's a lot of fun to be with.'

'That's it — Nigel Westwood. You watch it, my girl. I hear he's got quite a reputation. And he was very keen on Sara Calvert while he was on the mend. Are you sure he's not two-timing you?'

'I'm sure he isn't. Anyway, it doesn't really bother me. There's nothing serious between us.'

'They all say that,' said Penny darkly. 'Next thing they're walking up the aisle. Mind you, I'm inclined to believe you. Nigel Westwood isn't the marrying type, he's just a playboy. Love 'em and leave 'em type.'

Juliet didn't answer. She pushed her chair against the table.

'Fancy your not meeting Dr Kent yet,' Penny went on. 'And you on Melrose.'

'It's only my second day,' said Juliet, 'and I must dash.' For a moment she'd been on the verge of telling Penny why she was in such a hurry, but the moment passed, and she was glad she hadn't given in to the impulse. Penny was a very active shoot on the hospital grapevine, and Juliet didn't want her mother's operation talked about and discussed.

She hurried from the dining-room, squeezing past a group of nurses gazing at the day's menu on the board. Someone called out to her, and she turned to acknowledge it, at the same time feeling herself collide with a broad chest in a white coat.

'Oh, I'm sorry——'

A pair of brown eyes looked into her own deep blue ones. 'Don't mention it.' His voice matched his eyes and his mop of dark curly hair. His hand had grasped her arm to steady her. 'In a hurry?' he murmured.

'Yes, I am.'

'Mustn't be late back on duty, must we?'

'I'm not——' Juliet began. But she didn't have to explain. She'd apologised, hadn't she? She twisted out of his grasp and pushed through the swing doors. She had ten minutes, that was all, to see that her mother was safely tucked up on Hunter Ward, and reassured that everything was going to be all right. Because it was going to be all right, wasn't it? It had to be, if only for her father's sake.

She glanced briefly back as the doors closed behind her, and was a little surprised to see the brown-eyed doctor still gazing after her. He had to be fairly new, she decided. She'd never seen him before. Not a houseman — he seemed too confident to be a mere houseman. A registrar, then. She wondered briefly about Penny's talk of Dr Kent. Then the lift came, and she hurried inside, and within minutes was pushing open the doors to the gynaecological ward on the third floor.

Hunter Ward, and others, was named after one of the hospital's benefactors, way back in the 1960s. Riverside General had been built as an overflow hospital for Tewkesbury and Gloucester and surrounding areas.

Since then there had been several extensions built, a
new accident and emergency unit, and a radiotherapy
centre. Locals didn't always call it Riverside; it was
often referred to as Yonder, from the large village on its
doorstep.

After visiting once with her mother, while still at
school, Juliet had fallen in love with the hospital, and
had vowed there and then to do her nursing training at
Riverside. She was now coming to the end of her second
year, and only yesterday had been transferred from
Bassett, the male surgical ward. That was where she
had met Nigel, in one of the amenity side-wards. Nigel,
with his charming smile, his sophisticated way of talking, his ——

'Did you want something, Nurse?'

Juliet was jolted from her reverie. She gave Sister
what she hoped was a confident smile.

'It's my mother, Sister. She was to be admitted at ten
o'clock. Sister said I could come in my coffee break to
say hello to her and see that she's all right.'

Sister frowned. 'Is that an implication that we're not
looking after her properly?' Then she smiled. 'I quite
understand. What's her name?'

'Avery — Irene Avery.'

'Oh, yes, the D and C for tomorrow. Well, the
doctor's with her at the moment, although he shouldn't
be long. She's in Room B. You'd better wait in the
visitors' room. I expect your father is still there.'

'Oh, good.'

Sister smiled again and disappeared into the ward,
into one of the four-bedded rooms. Juliet could see her
father through the half-open door of the visitors' room.
He was gazing at a print of unrealistic mountains
against a brilliant blue sky.

'Dad, I didn't expect to find you still here.'

He turned with a vaguely surprised smile, and she
hugged him.

'I'm waiting to take her clothes. The doctor came just
as she was settling in. He seems all right, but very

young. Do you really think he'll be capable of doing the operation? He didn't look more than twenty.'

'Oh, Dad! I don't expect he's the consultant, or even the registrar — they do the operations. He's probably a junior doctor, come to take details.'

'I see. He's qualified?'

'Of course. You mustn't worry, Dad. I'm sure everything will be quite straightforward. It's a very minor operation, really. Just a scrape and snipping off a polyp.'

'You make it sound so simple, Juliet,' said Douglas Avery, sinking into a chair. 'I don't know anything about it. And your mother was very worried this morning. It's a long time since she was in hospital.'

'I know — before I was born. That's why I asked Sister if I could slip up here to see her.' She glanced at her watch. 'Although if that doctor doesn't go soon I shan't have time.'

'You can't wait?'

'This is my coffee break. I just didn't expect the doctor to see her quite so soon.' Juliet went to the doorway and looked along the ward, just as a doctor left one room and entered another.

'I think he's gone,' she said to her father. 'But I'd better check first.'

'Let me know,' said Douglas. 'I have to get to the bank.'

'They'll manage without you,' said Juliet, and went into the ward, striding confidently along as though she belonged there. No one seemed to be around. She reached Room B and went inside. Curtains were drawn around a bed near the window. One bed was empty, the sheets rumpled; an elderly lady was asleep in another. And in the remaining bed a grey-haired woman was busy knitting, listening to the radio through headphones. She barely glanced at Juliet as she crossed the room to the curtained bed. This had to be her mother's bed, she surmised, and the doctor had forgotten to draw back the curtains.

She had taken the curtain in one hand when she heard a man's voice.

'I wouldn't say genetic, Mrs Avery. Possibly familial. And of course, there are some conditions which are more prevalent among childless women like yourself.' Papers rattled, and Juliet drew back. The doctor was still here; she ought to leave. But suppose Sister saw her go? While she hesitated, the doctor continued.

'I see from your notes that the treatment for your infertility was never successful. But you have an adopted daughter.'

That's me, thought Juliet. He's referring to me. Her mother said something in a low voice, which she didn't catch.

'Of course,' said the doctor. 'But difficult to be sure, since your mother died quite young, and you had no brothers or sisters.'

What's he talking about? thought Juliet indignantly. Hasn't he read the notes properly? Of course her mother had had a sister — Elaine. She waited for her mother to deny this statement, but all remained quiet.

'So there we are,' he went on, and his voice seemed to carry more than ever. Juliet was sure everyone could hear, and was listening. 'Without any information about your mother, we can't surmise anything. Not that it matters, it's a very minor operation, but we shall have a look at the polyp under a microscope. That's routine, and I don't for a minute expect there to be any complications. Now, if I could just —— '

He's going to be ages, thought Juliet desperately, suddenly realising she'd been standing with her hands clenched together, and her eyes screwed tightly as if to hear better. I'll have to go back to Melrose or Sister will kill me!

Still stunned by what she'd overheard, she walked blindly from the room and through the ward to the visitors' room. Her father was looking out of the window, but he turned as she came in.

'Is she all right? Can I fetch her clothes?'

'I was wrong. The doctor's still with her.' Juliet stared at him, a puzzled frown on her face.

'Is something wrong, Juliet?' He came towards her.

'I don't know,' she said. 'The doctor must have misread the notes. But Mother should have corrected him, and she didn't.'

'What are you talking about, Juliet? What about your mother?'

'Ah, Mr Avery, you can go and see your wife now, and collect her clothes. I'm sorry you've been kept waiting so long. You've got the leaflet about visiting times, haven't you?' Sister glanced at Juliet. 'Are you going in with him?'

'No, I haven't really got time — I'll come this afternoon, I've got a split shift —— ' Juliet hurried past Sister out of the room. Her father was standing by the ward doors, looking bemused. Juliet gave him a quick wave and almost ran down to the lifts. She heard Sister's firm voice giving him directions, then the lift arrived and she stepped inside.

Sister Robinson was at the nurses' station, talking to one of the first-year nurses, when Juliet arrived back on the ward. She motioned for her to stay while continuing her instructions.

'Nurse Herbert is going to teach Donna how to flush her Hickman catheter. I want you to watch her very carefully, because afterwards I shall ask you about it. Right, off you go.'

'Yes, Sister.' The junior nurse scuttled off to Room F, where Jill Herbert, a third-year nurse, was obviously waiting. Sister turned to Juliet.

'Have you seen a Hickman catheter flushed out with heparin yet, Nurse Avery?'

Juliet, trying to collect her senses after the unthinkable revelation she'd overheard on Hunter Ward, shook her head. Sister didn't appear to be aware of her distracted expression, and went on talking.

'Of course you haven't — this is only your second day. Well, you'll have a chance in a couple of days when it's done again. I shan't go into the details now.'

'You're talking about Donna, in the single room,' said Juliet.

'That's right—Donna Hazell. Acute lymphocytic leukaemia—ALL for short. We don't get many here,
because they're mostly children who are affected. Donna
had her twentieth birthday about a month ago. She's
doing very well, considering her age; she's tolerated the
chemotherapy extremely well—lost her hair, of course,
but that should be temporary—and we hope she's going
into remission.' She smiled at Juliet. 'You're interested
in blood diseases?'

'I'm interested in all medical subjects.'

'Good. I called you over because I want you to look
after the new lady. Mrs Cole——' Sister opened a folder
on the desk '—was admitted this morning into Room
G.'

'The single room next to Donna.'

'For the time being. There's every chance she may go
to Intensive Care if she deteriorates.'

'What's wrong with her?' asked Juliet, remembering
the thin, dark-haired woman who had arrived on a
stretcher just before she went for her coffee break. The
woman had groaned a lot as if in pain.

'We've got an idea, but we're not sure. The doctor
will be here soon. She's in a lot of pain, and is extremely
anxious about her condition.'

'That's not surprising. Most patients are.'

Sister smiled. 'Mrs Cole has more reason than most
to be anxious. Her legs have become paralysed.' She
handed the file to Juliet. 'I want you to remember that
every sound, every bright light, every touch will be
extremely painful for her. It will test your nursing ability
to make her comfortable without hurting her.'

'I'll do my best.' Juliet picked up the orange folder
and walked down to Room G at the far end of the ward.
There were two single rooms at each end of the ward,
reserved for patients who needed isolation, or just
extreme quiet, away from the hustle and bustle that
usually surrounded the main parts of the ward.

The pale blue vertical blind in G was half closed to
cut out the sun, and the room was refreshingly cool.
Mrs Cole lay with her eyes closed, unnaturally still.

Remembering what Sister had said, Juliet closed the
door behind her carefully, and trod softly towards the
bed. Mrs Cole opened her eyes and gave Juliet a faint
smile.

'How are you, Mrs Cole?' asked Juliet quietly. 'I'm
Nurse Avery.' She didn't whisper, because that could
be more irritating than talking.

'A little better, thank you.'

'How's the pain?'

'Not so bad. Still some in my back. But it's my legs
I'm worried about — they feel like lumps of concrete. Do
they think it could be polio? I asked my own doctor
when he came early this morning, but he wouldn't tell
me.'

'Have you been vaccinated against polio?' Juliet laid
the opened folder on the long cupboard under the
window.

'Is that the sugar lumps? Yes, I had those, a long
time ago. But if it isn't polio, what is it?' Mrs Cole's
voice rose with anxiety, and Juliet rested a hand on her
arm.

'I'm sure the doctor will tell you when he comes to
see you.'

'Is he coming soon? I've got an awful feeling this
deadness will creep up and up and kill me — like
Socrates. He took — '

'Hemlock. Yes, I know, Mrs Cole. I'm sure you
haven't been eating hemlock stalks instead of celery,
have you?'

Mrs Cole gave a quick smile. 'No, of course not. It's
just — '

'Would you like me to help you get more comfortable?' asked Juliet. 'Do you want to sit up more? A
drink?'

Mrs Cole shook her head. 'No — please — I'd rather
not be moved. The pain's almost gone, for the first time
in three days. Three days! I thought I'd put a disc out
or something, then yesterday my legs started to feel
quite strange, and when I woke this morning — — my

husband was really worried, he fetched the doctor——
Nurse Avery, I'm so scared!'

'Please, don't get so upset,' said Juliet gently. 'The
doctor will be here soon, and I'm sure——' She turned
as the door behind her opened, and the curly-haired
doctor she'd seen briefly in the dining-room came softly
towards the bed. He gave Juliet a quick appraising
glance before turning to the patient. Juliet handed him
the folder, which contained only basic notes and the
GP's letter, which he read quickly. As he did so, Juliet
was able to study him without his being aware of it.

She knew his eyes were a deep velvety brown, and
she knew they were soft and kind. His mouth was kind
too, sensitive but firm. His skin was tanned, his jaw
determined. And his eyelashes were long and curling.
She hadn't had time to notice them before.

I do like curling eyelashes in a man, she found herself
thinking, and couldn't help the faint flush that rose in
her cheeks. What am I doing? What would Nigel think?
Had she told the truth when she'd said there was
nothing serious between them? She had to admit it, she
liked Nigel a lot, and the feeling seemed to be mutual.
But I can still admire other men, she told herself
defiantly. A pity Nigel hasn't got long curling eyelashes.

'Were you planning on leaving us, Nurse—Avery?'
The doctor's voice broke in on her thoughts. He knew
her name! Then she noticed his gaze on her name
badge.

'Leaving you?' She glanced briefly at his lapel badge.
Dr D Kent. So this was the eligible Dr Kent that Penny
had mentioned.

'Back into the ward. Because I shall probably need
some help here when I examine Mrs Cole, as she finds
it difficult to move.'

'I wasn't planning on going anywhere, Dr Kent,' said
Juliet. 'I've been told to stay here as long as I'm needed.'

'Good. We'll start first with some basic information,
Mrs Cole. It's Roberta, isn't it?' He sat carefully on a
stool by the bed.

'Everyone calls me Bobbie,' she told him.

He grinned, showing attractive, if slightly uneven, white teeth. Makes him look more sexy, thought Juliet, and wondered what had come over her today. She tried not to look at him as he talked.

Dr Kent was very thorough in his questioning, quickly eliciting that Mrs Cole was thirty-four, married with three children, and had suffered a bout of flu three weeks previously. At this information he nodded, and wrote something in large letters on the page. Juliet, peering over his broad, white-coated shoulder, read the words ?GUILLAIN-BARRE. She didn't know what it meant; she had never heard it before.

It was while the doctor was asking Bobbie for details of her family that Juliet suddenly remembered her mother up on Hunter Ward. And when Bobbie began to tell Dr Kent about her sister, who had a new baby, Juliet recalled the strange statement the houseman had made, and her mother's silence. It was a puzzle that just would not go away.

She was so engrossed in her thoughts that Dr Kent had to speak to her twice before she heard his request to help him move Bobbie Cole so that he could examine her. It was painful for the woman, and Juliet tried to comfort her, but the doctor was still frowning as he concluded the examination. He straightened up, and Juliet tidied the sheets.

'What is it, Doctor?' asked Bobbie, grimacing as she tried to move.

'I'm almost certain I know what it is, Bobbie.' He wrote on the chart. 'But to confirm my diagnosis I need to do some tests. One is a lumbar puncture — that means taking fluid from around your spinal cord. I shall come back this afternoon to do it. I want you to get some sleep, if you can. And you can have more painkillers if you need them.'

'Polio?' asked Bobbie in a small voice. He smiled.

'I'm pretty sure it isn't.' He left the room, indicating to Juliet to follow him. As the door closed behind them he turned to her, frowning.

'Do you really find it so difficult to keep your mind on your work, Nurse Avery?'

Hot colour suffused her cheeks. 'I'm sorry, I had—something on my mind.' She couldn't look at him, but she was still aware that he was studying her.

Then he said, 'Just try to concentrate on the patients. That's what you're here for.'

She nodded mutely, and followed him meekly back to the nurses' station. Oh, dear, she hadn't made a very good impression on the fabulous Dr Kent. What would he think of her? She tossed her short black hair. Did it really matter?

Douglas Avery had gone in to the bank as usual, after collecting Irene's clothes, so Juliet knew he wouldn't be visiting during the afternoon. He could have asked for time off, she reflected, and would probably have been given it, but he was just not assertive enough. Just as he could have received promotion over the years, but had always been turned down in favour of someone younger. She sighed. He'd never be bank manager now, and probably wouldn't have wanted to be.

As Juliet intended to visit her mother during her split shift, there was no point in going home. Instead she had lunch in the dining-room and went along to the hospital library. There she chose a textbook on medical diseases and took it along to the lounge in the nurses' residence. It was deserted and quiet, and she soon became absorbed in the chapter on leukaemia. The girl in the single room, Donna Hazell, had leukaemia, but was going into remission. The same age as myself, thought Juliet as she read, and tried to imagine what it would be like.

She glanced at her watch. Almost time for visiting. Her mother would be pleased to see her. She hadn't been a patient for over twenty years, since she'd had the barrage of undignified tests and minor operations that had led to nothing but disappointment. And then her younger sister, Elaine, ten years younger, Irene had told Juliet——

The door opened. 'Studying?' A third-year nurse came in and turned on the radio. Pop music filled the room. It was nearly time. Juliet closed the book and stood up.

'I hope I haven't driven you away,' said the other nurse, opening a thick textbook on paediatrics. 'I find music helps me to study.'

'Some music,' Juliet agreed. 'I have to go, anyway.'

She stood outside the lifts in the hospital's main entrance with other visitors. They were armed with flowers and fruit and magazines and wore an air of expectancy. Someone came and stood behind her, and she glanced back instinctively, her cheeks immediately flushing.

'I thought you were off duty?' murmured Dr Kent into her ear. The visitors looked at her curiously.

'I have an appointment on Hunter Ward.'

'Appointment? As a patient?' he suggested, and she flushed redder still. Was he intentionally embarrassing her?

'I'm visiting my mother. She's been admitted for a D and C.'

'Ah, that explains your preoccupation this morning. I'm sorry if I was a bit brusque with you. I didn't realise you were worrying about your mother.'

'I wasn't really—it was something else——' The doors opened and the visitors surged forward. Juliet found herself squeezed next to Dr Kent, and was acutely aware of the pressure of his body, and his faint aroma of spearmint and Savlon. She was also suddenly aware of her own racing pulse.

By the third floor, many of the visitors had disembarked. The doors opened and Juliet stepped out.

'*Au revoir*,' said Dr Kent, his brown eyes crinkling, and she smiled at him. He wasn't so bad, after all. The lift carried on upwards and Juliet followed the other visitors into Hunter Ward.

In Room B, Irene Avery was sitting by her bed, wrapped in a warm blue dressing-gown, a magazine on the counterpane in front of her. A smile lit up her plain face as Juliet approached. The woman in the next bed, busily knitting when Juliet had called earlier, glanced at her. Juliet kissed her mother's cool cheek.

'This is my daughter,' Irene called to the woman. 'She's a nurse here.' Juliet could hear the pride in her voice.

The woman nodded. 'Yes, I saw her this morning when she came.' She turned back to her visitors.

Irene stared at Juliet. 'You came this morning? I didn't see you.'

'No — no, I couldn't wait, it was my coffee break. The doctor was with you.' And suddenly she was hearing again the doctor's words, 'and you had no. . .sisters,' and feeling the shock she had experienced then. Surely the doctor had made a misake? She opened her mouth to ask her mother why he'd said that, and just as abruptly closed it again, realising that this wasn't the time or the place to discuss private family matters.

But I shall find out, Juliet promised herself. I shan't be able to rest until I do.

The hour went slowly. There was really very little to talk about, since they'd seen each other at breakfast, so conversation became desultory once Irene had told Juliet about the other patients — the hysterectomies, the ovarian cyst as big as a football, and the girl who had come to be sterilised and was found to be pregnant.

The bell rang, the visitors shifted their chairs, everyone was kissing and saying goodbye.

'I'm not sure I shall be able to come tonight,' said Juliet. 'I'm on duty. And anyway, Dad will be here.'

'You will try, though, won't you? But don't worry if you can't manage it. Sister said I may be first on the list tomorrow morning.'

'Oh, good. I'll try to slip over if I get a spare minute. But I'll come when I finish at five, in any case.' Juliet kissed her and left. The other visitors were leaving last messages, and collecting used nightclothes in carrier bags.

Juliet was passing the nurses' station when an idea came to her. It would be so simple to check if the doctor

had made a mistake in reading her mother's notes. And
it could prevent a lot of embarrassment to everyone
concerned. A ward clerk was fixing pathology and X-
ray reports into folders, taking very little notice of the
visitors as they left. Juliet paused beside her. She was in
uniform; could she pull it off?

'Excuse me — it's about Mrs Avery. I wondered —— '

The ward clerk glanced at her and stuck in another
report. 'It's no use asking me — I don't know the
patients. I've only come for the afternoon because
Sheila's off sick. You'll have to ask Sister. She's in the
office with Dr Price. Better still, why don't you look at
the notes?'

'That's what I was going to suggest.' Juliet ran her
fingers over the files in the trolley. They were in room
order, A, B — Smart — Avery —— Her hands shook as
she drew out the file and turned back the cover.

Sister was leaving her office. Juliet thrust back the file
and hurried down the ward. Sister smiled at her.

'Been to see your mother, Nurse Avery?'

'Yes, Sister. She's fine.' Juliet hurried from the ward,
hoping the ward clerk hadn't overheard Sister's words
and become suspicious.

At five o'clock she returned to Melrose. She'd spent the
rest of the afternoon trying to find out all she could
about leukaemia, and the funny disease Dr Kent
thought Bobbie Cole had. But she didn't know where to
find it in the rows of medical books in the nursing school
library. It did seem, however, that Donna Hazell, the
girl with leukaemia, stood a very good chance of being
cured if she had a bone-marrow transplant. Juliet felt
quite pleased about this; the girl was her own age,
twenty, and, although she'd seen her only a few times,
she felt drawn to her cheerful, intelligent personality.

She entered Sister's office just as she was giving a
final briefing to Staff Nurse Target, who had also worked
a split shift. Sister called Juliet to her. 'I want you to
take over from Nurse Calvert when they've finished in
Room G with Mrs Cole.' She glanced at her watch.

'That lumbar puncture seems to be taking them a long time.'

The lumbar puncture. Dr Kent. Juliet couldn't understand why she suddenly felt suspicious of Sara Calvert. The third-year nurse had worked with Juliet on Bassett Ward, where Nigel had been a patient, and she'd never felt uneasy about her then. And all Penny Rogers's talk about Sara and Nigel — well, she was just starting a rumour, wasn't she? Wanted to make me feel jealous, thought Juliet. It wouldn't work. I'm not the jealous type, she told herself. So why did she feel like this now? It couldn't be Dr Kent; she hardly knew him, she'd only spoken to him three times, and then briefly. No, it wasn't Dr Kent. Although Sara Calvert was very attractive, with ash-blonde hair and an enviable figure. She was tall, too, inches taller than Juliet, who was a petite five feet three inches.

Men do prefer blondes, she thought, and unconsciously pushed back a strand of her own urchin-cut black hair.

Sister was telling Wendy Target about the blood results on Donna Hazell. 'She'll be home soon, I should imagine, on maintenance chemotherapy. Then it will just be a matter of finding a suitable donor for bone marrow.'

'She's having a transplant, then?' put in Juliet.

'You still here?' remarked Sister. 'Will you please go along to Room G and see what's keeping them? Nurse Calvert should be off duty.'

'Yes, Sister.' Juliet left the office and hurried towards the far end of the ward. And, just leaving Room G, came Sara Calvert and Dr Kent, pushing a littered trolley before them. At least, Sara was ostensibly pushing it, but Dr Kent's hand seemed to be on top of hers, helping her to guide it along the passage between the rooms. Sara was looking up at him as he said something, then she gave a long, shrill laugh, showing her perfect white teeth.

She shouldn't be laughing like that outside Mrs Cole's room, thought Juliet crossly. It's painful for the poor woman. And Dr Kent should reprimand her for it. He very quickly told me off because I was a bit absent-minded. Although he did apologise, she reminded herself.

She went to meet them, hoping her expression didn't reveal her feelings. 'All done?' she asked brightly. Sara glanced at Dr Kent, but he was looking at Juliet and smiling.

'All finished,' he said. 'Let me tell you about her. She was given pethidine cover while it was done, and is resting now. She's written up for dihydrocodeine four-hourly.' He glanced at his watch. 'Seven o'clock for her next dose. Whatever you do, don't wait until she's in pain. And let me know if she needs anything stronger.' He moved aside so Juliet could pass.

'Heavens,' exclaimed Sara, still standing by them with the trolley, 'I didn't realise it was so late! And I've got a date at seven!' She flashed her teeth at Dr Kent, saying lightly, 'Doesn't time fly when you're having fun?'

Juliet went into Room G to see how Bobbie Cole was, but there was little she could do. The woman was peacefully sleeping, had obviously been washed and made presentable by Sara, and wore a fresh pink cotton nightdress.

Juliet had to admit that, despite her flippant manner and constant flirting, Sara Calvert was a good nurse. She closed the blind and left the room. When she got back to the office, both Dr Kent and Sara had gone, and Staff Nurse Target was anxious to start the drugs round with her.

At seven o'clock Wendy went to supper, leaving Juliet on the ward with the auxiliary. Juliet sat down to read the report. Someone entered the room behind her.

'Are they all ready for visitors, Mrs Ashwin?' asked Juliet, without turning her head.

'I'm sure they are,' came Dr Kent's voice in reply. She jumped, her face pink with embarrassment.

'Oh—I didn't expect you to come round again. I thought you'd be off duty.'

'On call.' He sat on the corner of the desk and swung his leg. His brown eyes surveyed her. 'Is Bobbie Cole all right?'

'She roused not long ago, and Staff gave her her dihydrocodeine.'

'And how was your mother?'

'Oh, you remembered. She's fine. It's only a minor op, after all, and snipping off a polyp, so I don't think I shall bother to go up tonight—we're far too busy here, and anyway, my father will be there, and I don't really think she's expecting me, so I'll wait until tomorrow——'

'Hey, hey, I wasn't expecting a speech.' His brown eyes twinkled.

'Sorry—I got carried away. I suppose I feel a bit guilty.'

'Guilty?' He was watching her intently and she looked away. 'Why are you so worried about her if it's only a minor op?'

'I suppose I'm more worried about myself, if that makes sense.'

'It doesn't. Please explain.'

'I don't think I can. It's confusing—and I don't think my mother would want me to——' Juliet swallowed and looked up at him. He was looking very serious. 'Tell me, Dr Kent, I expect you know all the other doctors—the housemen, the registrars, I'm not sure which one it was, but he went to see my mother as soon as she was admitted——'

'Whose firm would that be?' he interrupted.

'Mr Graveney.'

He screwed up his eyes. 'That would be—let me see—the registrar's female, I hardly know her. Carol——'

'It was a man.'

'Warner—Phil Warner. What's he done?'

'He hasn't done anything. But Dr Kent, you obviously know him, would you say he was capable of misreading a patient's notes?'

'Depends on who wrote them!' said Dr Kent, grinning.

Juliet nibbled a fingernail. 'It didn't make sense, you see. I assumed he'd made a mistake, but suppose he hadn't? Suppose what he read out to my mother was the truth?'

'You're right, it doesn't make sense.' Dr Kent eased himself off the desk and sat in a chair next to her. 'Come on now, if it's bothering you so much you'd better get it off your chest. Tell Uncle David all about it.'

CHAPTER TWO

A SOFT giggle escaped Juliet. Uncle David! She'd never had an uncle like Dr Kent. Come to that, she had only one uncle, her father's brother Eric, and she hardly ever saw him. No men in her life, really, not even her natural father, because he'd gone away, emigrated, so she knew very little about men. Perhaps Dr Kent *was* an uncle; he'd be a nice uncle, she was sure.

She sighed. 'I don't really think I can tell you—it's so private, you see. Well, if Dr Warner *was* reading it correctly, then that makes it even more private than ever, because it would mean my mother's been lying, she must have some secret to hide. And really, I don't know you very well, do I?'

There was a pause. He seemed to be scrutinising her, and she felt her colour rise.

'Tell me, Nurse J Avery—and what does the J stand for, anyway?'

'Juliet.'

'Ah, Juliet. Tell me, Juliet, would you hesitate to tell your own doctor this problem that's worrying you to death?'

'No, of course not. He'd probably know, anyway. And if he didn't—well, it's all confidential, isn't it, in doctors' surgeries?'

'Can't you trust me enough to keep it between just the two of us?'

She looked into his brown eyes. They were watching her intently, with a look that disconcerted her and excited her at the same time.

She nodded. 'All right, I'll tell you. I was adopted when my own mother died a few days after I was born. That's what I was told.'

David Kent nodded slowly. 'I'm sure there's more.'

'My natural mother was my mother's younger sister,

so my mother's really my aunt, but I've always called
her Mum. She told me this when I was very small, so
I've always known my real mother didn't just give me
away.'

'And your natural father?'

'It seems he couldn't cope. My parents were more
than willing to look after me, since my mother was
infertile, so that's what happened. Eventually my real
father emigrated to New Zealand. I've never seen him.'

'It all sounds a very satisfactory state of affairs to me,'
said Dr Kent. 'Tell me where Phil Warner comes into
it.'

'My mother was admitted this morning on Hunter
Ward, and I dashed up during my coffee break to see
her.'

He nodded. 'I watched you hurtle from the dining-
room. You resembled some nervous leprechaun, fleeing
from human gaze.'

'A leprechaun? What made you think I was Irish?'

'Aren't you? No Irish blood in you at all? With that
raven hair and eyes like gentians?'

She couldn't help laughing. 'You should have been a
poet! "Raven hair and eyes like gentians", indeed!'

He leaned towards her. '"And still she slept an azure-
lidded sleep",' he quoted.

'Azure? You were talking about gentians.'

He made a wry expression. 'I don't know any poems
offhand that have gentians in them. Or raven-black
hair, for that matter. That was a line from Keats, in
case you didn't know.'

'I didn't. But aren't we getting away from the
subject?'

'You're right, we are. But I still suspect you have
Irish blood in you.'

'I wish I knew. If my aunt Elaine was really my
mother, then I don't. But after I heard Dr Warner
saying that to my mother about not having any
sisters——'

'This is what he read from her notes, I take it?'

'Obviously. I didn't realise anyone was still with her.

I thought the doctor had forgotten to draw back the
curtain, and I was just about to do it when I heard his
voice. And he referred quite clearly to the notes someone
had taken, information my mother must have given
them. She must have done, because she didn't deny it
when he said she had no brothers or sisters!' Juliet
turned anguished eyes on him.

'So Elaine wasn't her sister?' said David Kent quietly.

'It all points to that. Oh, David —— ' and the name
slipped out before she realised it ' — if Elaine wasn't my
mother's sister, who was she? And what does that make
me?'

David Kent sat back in his chair. 'I think, before you
start leaping to conclusions, you ought to ask your
mother about it. You may be getting it all wrong. You
overheard something; did you stay to listen to any
more?'

She shook her head. 'I was too shocked. I just left. I
didn't see her until this afternoon, and I couldn't ask
her then, not just before her operation. It would worry
her. And she's already worried in case the polyp turns
out to be something worse.'

David nodded. 'Then you'll just have to wait until
she's over it. What about your father? Haven't you
thought of asking him?'

'No. I suppose I could, once Mum's had her operation — he won't be so worried then. Dr Kent, I don't
know whether I should ask them at all. It's like —
accusing them of lying. And they've been such good
parents to me.'

He laid a hand on hers. His touch was warm and
encouraging. 'I'm afraid I can't advise you there. You'll
have to make up your own mind.' He stood up and
smiled down at her. 'Shall we go and check Mrs Cole?'

The evening proved to be extremely busy, and Juliet
found it impossible to slip up to Hunter again. A woman
had been admitted with acute pancreatitis, desperately
ill. Drips had been put up, pethidine given, stomach
tubes passed. Juliet had managed to grab a cup of coffee

and a sandwich, but had been reluctant to leave Wendy
Target virtually alone on the ward, so she had hurried
back after ten minutes.

At least, she consoled herself as she slipped on her
jacket, her mother wasn't really expecting her. And
surely it would be nicer for her parents to be alone
together, wouldn't it?

Light was fading as she wheeled her cycle around the
side of their semi-detached house in Yonder, and
propped it against the fence. She was too exhausted to
put it away. Too bad if rain had been forecast.

Douglas Avery was watching snooker on television.
Snooker was his hobby, and he usually made a weekly
visit to a snooker club nearby, with his next-door
neighbour, Bill Austin. Juliet made a hot drink for them
both, and took them through to the sitting-room.

'Was Mum all right?' she asked, sitting down and
taking off her shoes. What bliss! Her father took his
drink from the table near him.

'I thought you were going to call in,' he remarked.
'Your mother was expecting you.'

Juliet couldn't help feeling a little exasperated. 'I said
I'd try, but we were just far too busy. I didn't even have
time for a proper supper.'

He nodded and his gaze returned to the final frame of
snooker. 'Your mother was a bit put out — oh, good
shot! — she said you were a bit offhand with her this
afternoon. She thought she'd upset you in some way.'

'No — no, of course not!' Juliet spoke too quickly. She
drained her mug and stood up. 'I'm desperately tired.
I'm on early again tomorrow, so I think I'll get an early
night.'

She kissed her father and left him on the edge of his
seat.

'Goodnight, dear.' He spoke absently. Juliet slowly
climbed the stairs. She *was* tired, but it was a tiredness
of mind as well as body. Tomorrow, once her mother
was over the small operation, she would have to think
again about what she'd overheard. She must have made

a mistake herself. She hadn't waited long enough for her mother's reply.

As her eyes closed in sleep she knew that hadn't been the case at all.

Next morning, on the ward, the pancreatitis patient was only slightly improved, and Bobbie Cole was, unfortunately, a little worse. Doctors seemed to be coming and going all morning, so it wasn't until she was sent to coffee that Juliet had time to think of her mother. She decided to forgo the coffee, and rushed up to Hunter Ward, just as another patient was being wheeled back from Theatre, drip held aloft by the nurse. Sister came out and took charge, and Juliet was left standing outside, wondering who she could ask. Finally, a third-year nurse came bustling out and saw her.

'I know you're busy,' Juliet began. 'Has Mrs Avery been down yet?'

'Avery? Oh yes, been back ages. Hey, aren't you ——?'

'Yes, she's my mother. Is she all right?'

'I can't let you in, we're in the middle of a big list, and Sister would kill me. She was only a D and C wasn't she?'

'And a polyp. She was worried about the polyp,' Juliet explained.

'Oh, right. Well, I haven't heard anything to the contrary, so I presume that's what it was. You'd better check with Sister, but I should imagine she'll be home tomorrow.'

'That's a relief. Thanks.'

'She can have visitors tonight.' The nurse disappeared into Sister's office and closed the door.

Juliet hurried back to Melrose feeling a bit happier. Dr Kent was with the new patient, and Sister sent her to see if he needed any help. But he had finished whatever he'd been doing, so Juliet just tidied the bed and put a few things away.

'Keep an eye on the drip,' said David Kent automatically, as they left the bedside. He looked exhausted, and

Juliet had to subdue the sudden urge she felt to stroke his drawn face.

'You look tired,' she said quietly. He gave her a gentle smile.

'You're so sweet. Yes, I was on call all last night. We had an acute keto-acidosis on Folliott.' Folliott was the male medical ward. Juliet wasn't quite sure what keto-acidosis was, so she just nodded, reminding herself to look it up.

'Fortunately, I'm off duty at two,' the doctor went on. 'I shall probably go to bed for the afternoon, and think of you lot working.'

Juliet couldn't understand why she suddenly felt bereft.

'Lucky you!' she said. 'But how can you be thinking of us while you're asleep? Surely you don't dream about us?'

'I think I may dream of leprechauns, with blue eyes and raven-black hair. How's your mother, by the way?'

He had changed the subject so adroitly that Juliet could only stare at him.

'She's had the D and C. Everything straightforward, and she can probably go home tomorrow.'

'That's good. Have you thought about what you plan to do?'

At every spare moment, she wanted to say. Instead she said, 'I think I shall talk to my father first. Then, if I did get it wrong, my mother won't need to know.'

He nodded. 'That's very wise. Don't forget to let me know what happens. Now, I think Sister's looking for you.'

Juliet hurried away, but she couldn't stop the warm glow that seemed to fill her. He *was* nice, he was really interested in her problem. She wished all the doctors were as caring as he was. Most of them ignored mere second-year nurses, unless they were incredibly attractive like Sara Calvert.

Melrose Ward was much quieter that afternoon. There was the low hum of visitors, the fresh smell of flowers

and fruit, and, not for the first time, Juliet found her
thoughts drifting away to David Kent, asleep in his
room. Room? Or flat? Or house? She had no idea
whether he lived in or out of the hospital. It didn't really
concern her, after all.

'How's your mother, Nurse Avery?' asked Sister
Robinson, as she approached the nurses' station where
Juliet was studying Bobbie Cole's test results. She
glanced up.

'She's fine, thank you, Sister. It was just a polyp, I
believe, and she should be home tomorrow.'

'That's wonderful! Look, we're a bit quiet at the
moment, so why don't you take an extra ten minutes on
your tea break and go and see her? I'm sure they were
far too busy this morning to let you.'

Juliet nodded. 'Thank you, Sister, I'd like that.'

Sister glanced at the file in Juliet's hand. 'Mrs Cole —
an interesting case.'

'I'd never heard of Guillain-Barré Syndrome before.
It seems to be quite serious.'

'Very serious. But it can vary from patient to patient.
Mrs Cole isn't one of the worst cases I've seen, by a
long chalk. She could be totally paralysed and on a
ventilator in Intensive Care, in which case it could be
months before she recovers. However, both Dr Kent
and Dr Whitfield are of the opinion that she may avoid
respiratory distress.'

'I do hope so,' said Juliet fervently. 'She's a nice
woman.'

Sister smiled. 'I hope that remark doesn't imply that
you wouldn't care so much if she was a nasty person.
I'm sure it doesn't. And I know what you mean. Off
you go now, for your break. Be back at four.'

She was being generous, thought Juliet as she looked
at her watch. She hurried to the lift.

There was still a lot of activity going on in Hunter
Ward, even though it was visiting hour. Many of the
patients were now attached to drips and drainage bags,
and nurses flitted to and fro. Sister was off duty, but the

staff nurse, a big, auburn-haired girl with freckles, agreed to let Juliet see her mother for a few minutes.

Juliet approached Room B warily. The other three patients had visitors, and bunches of flowers lay on the counterpanes. Irene Avery lay with her eyes closed, and for a moment Juliet hoped she would stay asleep so they didn't have to talk. Then a visitor laughed, and Irene opened her eyes. She stared at Juliet for a second, then struggled to a sitting position. Juliet reached out to help her.

'I didn't expect anyone until tonight,' said Irene, adjusting her floral nightdress.

Juliet kissed her. 'Sister said I could come, since it was only a minor operation. How are you? I came this morning, but they were awfully busy.'

'Like Paddy's market. I went down early — don't remember much about it.'

'Has the doctor been to see you?'

'I don't think so. But Sister's very pleased with me. She said everything went fine — no complications, just a polyp. Your father will be glad.'

'I'm glad too,' smiled Juliet.

'I can go home tomorrow, Doug can bring my clothes. Are you off duty now?'

'No, it's my tea break.'

'You've had your tea?'

'No, I came here first. I wanted to see you.' Juliet swallowed. How could she explain to her mother how she really felt? She had seen her, and now she wanted to go, before she gave in to an impulse and started asking her questions about Elaine.

'You'd better go, then. Get your tea,' said Irene. 'I shall be all right.'

'I should have brought you some flowers ——'

'Not worth it, if I'm going home tomorrow. Put some in the house.'

'Yes, I'll do that.'

There was really nothing to talk about. Juliet felt awkward, wishing she hadn't listened outside the curtains yesterday, and feeling a coward because she didn't

really want to face her mother's embarrassment. Perhaps there was an explanation for what she'd heard,
perhaps she was imagining the worst. Her father would
know. He'd tell her.

She said goodbye to her mother and went down to
tea.

She reached home at half-past five. Domino, their
elderly Dalmation, rushed to meet her, tail wagging
with excitement. Juliet hugged him and sent him into
the garden. Later, she'd take him for a walk, if her
father didn't have time.

It wasn't long before she heard Douglas's car draw
up on the short gravel drive. She tensed as she filled the
kettle, and checked the fridge for something for dinner.
All the way home, pedalling furiously, she had been
nerving herself for this confrontation.

Her father came in through the back door. 'Have you
seen her?' were his first words. 'Is she all right? I rang
the hospital at lunchtime.'

Juliet put a tea-bag in the pot. 'Yes, I've seen her.
Everything went well, and it was nothing serious. She
can come home tomorrow.'

'Tomorrow? That's a bit soon, isn't it?'

'It was only a minor operation, Dad. She'll be right
as rain in a couple of days. Anyway, you'll see her
tonight. You'll see what I mean.'

'I bought her some of her favourite fruit jellies.' He
laid a box on the kitchen counter. 'I thought she'd be in
for a week.'

'Dad——' Juliet hesitated. Her father turned back
and looked at her.

'Is something wrong? Something they didn't tell me?'

'No, Dad, it's nothing like that. Dad—I want to talk
to you.'

'That sounds ominous. I suppose you want to get
married. I thought it was old-fashioned to ask your
father.'

Juliet tried to laugh, but it came out rather strangled.

'Nothing to do with getting married. You go into the
sitting-room and I'll bring the tea.'

The sitting-room overlooked the street, and the lines
of horse-chestnut trees in bloom. Tiny white blossoms
patterned the pavement like confetti. They sat down
facing each other. Juliet's throat felt dry as she poured
the tea in silence.

'What's all this about?' asked her father, taking his
cup.

'Yesterday morning,' began Juliet, 'when we were
both on Hunter Ward waiting for the doctor to finish
talking to Mum.' She swallowed. 'You remember?'

'Yes,' Douglas nodded. 'Was it something the doctor
said?'

'In a way.' She told him what she had overheard.
There was silence in the room, an oppressive silence.
Juliet was waiting for her father's denial, as she had
waited for her mother's, but again, it didn't come. She
looked up.

'So the doctor didn't make a mistake?' she asked.
'Mum didn't have a sister called Elaine? She wasn't my
mother?'

Her father cleared his throat. He seemed unable to
look directly at her. 'I'm sorry you had to hear it this
way. But you're only partly right. Elaine was your
mother, as we always told you.'

'You always told me she was my mother's sister.
Why? Why did you need to tell me lies? I always knew
I was adopted, so why couldn't I have had the whole
truth? What was so dreadful that you couldn't tell me?
Was she a murderer or something?'

Angry tears pricked her eyes. Her father made a
gesture towards her.

'Please, Juliet — don't take it so hard! Of course we
should have told you everything — but your
mother — '

'Did she die? Did Elaine die? Or was that another
lie?'

Douglas spread his hands in resignation. 'Why
couldn't you have waited until your mother was home

to ask me all these things? I'm no good at this sort of thing. We don't know what happened to Elaine. She's never been traced. She abandoned you.'

A lump of ice settled in Juliet's stomach. The heat of her anger died away under this latest icy shock.

'Abandoned me? Like — like those cases you see in the newspapers? Baby found in public convenience? Or shop doorway? Or convent steps? Like that?'

Juliet's voice was rising; she knew she was losing control. Her father looked frightened.

'No, Juliet, it wasn't like that at all! Elaine just left you with us — and disappeared. She would never have left you at risk. She wasn't that kind of girl.'

'You met her?'

'No — actually I didn't. Juliet, it wasn't my idea that the whole truth should be kept from you. I was all for telling you everything about Elaine. Your mother felt it might make you insecure if you knew Elaine had just gone and left you like that.'

'And of course, Mother's word is law.' Douglas looked sheepish. 'All these years, Dad, I believed I'd actually got some roots of my own, roots in this family, even a natural father in New Zealand —— ' She broke off and looked questioningly at her father. He shook his head, his expression contrite. Juliet felt frustrated by his passiveness.

'I don't have a real father in New Zealand?' she said quietly.

'Elaine never said who your father was. The meeting between her and your mother was really quite brief —— '

Juliet stood up angrily and walked rigidly across to the window. This wasn't really happening, it was a dream, a nightmare, and she'd wake up soon and turn off the alarm and get ready for work. And it would be yesterday morning again, and she hadn't been up to Hunter Ward and eavesdropped on a conversation.

Outside, another blossom fell from a tree, to join the others on the pavement. It did resemble a church precinct after a wedding. A wedding. Had there been a wedding before her birth? Or was she —— ? Oh, everyone would argue that it didn't matter these days, it wasn't important.

I'd just like to know! she whispered to herself, barely aware of the tears sliding down her cheeks. She didn't bother to wipe them away. Her father came and put a hand on her shoulder. Her first instinct was to shrug it away in temper, but it wasn't his fault.

'I'm sorry,' he said, and she gave him a watery smile. 'Why don't you talk to your mother?' he asked. 'Perhaps I ought to warn her tonight that you know.'

She turned to face him. 'No! No, not at the hospital. I don't want to feel responsible if she has a fit of hysterics on the ward and can't come home tomorrow. No, I'll talk to her — later. There's no rush.'

Douglas smiled gently. He looked relieved. 'That's right. No point in rushing something like this.'

'Not after twenty years.' She forced a smile. 'Are you hungry?'

'Oh, not really. I'd like another cup of tea. Are you going out tonight?'

It was the last thing Juliet felt she wanted to do. 'I've got nothing planned. Nigel will probably ring.'

Douglas nodded and went to pour himself another cup of tea. Juliet went upstairs and sat on her bed. She felt strange, different. She wasn't the same Juliet Avery who had cycled to the hospital yesterday morning, blithe and carefree. Of course, her name was still Juliet Avery, but names meant nothing, did they? Who was she, really?

CHAPTER THREE

It was difficult, trying to pretend that everything was still the same. Juliet cooked them both a meal for which she had no appetite, and watched her father leave for the hospital in his blue Cavalier.

'Remember — nothing about what I've found out,' she warned him.

He nodded. 'I'll be diplomacy itself.' He kissed her and left. She went into the kitchen and tidied up, and then sat at the front window, watching people pass, hunched in her own disillusionment. She found it hard to understand how her parents could have deceived her all her life. If she hadn't gone into that room, heard that doctor talking. . . She might never have known. And that would undoubtedly have been for the best. But what was done was done. There was no going back. And she had a right to know the whole story.

The phone rang, and she rose lethargically and went to answer it.

'Julie?' She felt slight irritation at the abbreviation of her name. It was the one thing about Nigel she disliked. She tried to inject enthusiasm into her voice.

'Hello, Nigel. I thought you might ring.'

Nigel didn't appear to notice her lack of ardour, but went blithely on about having the house to himself for the weekend, so there was going to be a party, and he'd come and fetch her —

'Hang on, Nigel, you're rushing me. A party on Friday, you say, at your house?'

'It'll be great, Julie, I've got a lot of people I want you to meet, and there'll be lots to drink —— You are coming, aren't you? You must! I'm holding it for you ——'

'It is short notice.' Did she feel like a party right now?

She felt more like hiding in a corner and never coming out.

'You're not working, are you? If you are, get another nurse to do your shift for you—you can do that, can't you? And do you realise it's almost a week since I saw you?' His tone became low and intimate. 'I've missed you, Julie, darling. Have you missed me?'

'Of course.'

'I wish you didn't have to do that awful job, it takes up too much of your time, and I get jealous.'

'Jealous? Of what?'

'Of whom, you mean. All those virile young doctors. Don't forget, I saw a lot of them while I was bedridden and helpless. But you wouldn't go off with one of them, would you, sweet? Not when you have me.'

Why did she suddenly think of David Kent? Here she was, talking to Nigel, who, admittedly, was very attractive in a blatant sort of way, and all she could think of was David Kent's long eyelashes and his beautiful brown eyes! She couldn't help feeling guilty as she said smoothly, 'Why should I go off with one of them when I have you? How right you are!'

Nigel seemed to be lost for words for a moment. Then he said, almost aggressively, 'I couldn't bear it if you found someone else, if you were two-timing me. Tell me again you've missed me.'

'I've missed you.'

'And you'll come on Friday? Promise?'

'I'll come. I've got a half-day.'

'I'll pick you up at your house about six. Be ready—I can't wait to see you again!'

I'll have to ask him in, Juliet was thinking. Mum and Dad will want to meet him. Until now he had always picked her up from the hospital. Irene had often asked when she was going to bring him home. Would she understand how Juliet felt, with their tiny house and small garden, when the Westwoods lived in a great house with lots of land—Nigel had told her often enough—and all their friends were the same?

Of course, Nigel knew where she lived; he had always

brought her home since she couldn't afford to buy a car of her own just yet. But it had always been dark, and he had always been anxious to get back to Cheltenham, where he lived.

'Cheltenham?' her father had said. 'How did he get to be a patient at Yonder?'

'It was the nearest hospital to where he crashed his car. He was taking some friends home after a party in Great Malvern. Another car swerved on a patch of oil, Nigel tried to avoid him, and went off the road.'

They had accepted her word that Nigel hadn't been drunk. But he had been drinking, and deep inside she knew he had been partly to blame. A new car, a Porsche, showing off to friends, laughing, not really concentrating—The accident should have made him grow up a little. But now she couldn't help feeling disquiet at the way he talked about 'lots to drink'.

She'd have to get a taxi home. It would cost the earth, but it had to be safer than Nigel's Aston Martin. The Porsche had been a write-off. The only other alternative would be to ask her father to collect her from the party, and, at twenty, that would be too embarrassing for words! There was probably a night service bus, but she had no idea where she could catch it, or where it stopped in Yonder. No, it would have to be a taxi. And she hoped Nigel wouldn't take it as a slur on his driving.

She went to bed early, but she couldn't sleep. Visions of her mother's angry face when she told her what she knew changed into dreams of Nigel, back in hospital with bandages on his head, and David Kent with a Porsche, laughing and saying it was his now. When she woke, the sun was streaming through the window.

Her father was about to leave for work, by the time she had showered and dressed. He seemed to have forgotten the traumatic revelations of the previous evening, smiling and giving her a peck on the cheek as he left.

Juliet couldn't forget. But she couldn't stay angry with him. 'Don't forget,' she reminded him, 'ten o'clock at the hospital. You've got her things?'

He turned back. 'They're already in the car. We don't all stay in bed all day, you know.' And he grinned. It made him look younger.

'I'm sorry I yelled at you last night, Dad,' she said. He seemed surprised.

'It was quite understandable, dear. It must have been a shock to you.'

'Dad, would you object if I tried to find Elaine? Would Mum be upset?'

He considered this. 'I don't mind at all. You've every right to find your natural mother. But Irene — well, you know what she's like. She may take it as a slight on her ability as a mother. She always felt a failure, not being able to have a baby of her own. Of course, with all these test-tube babies now, and all the modern technology — it reminds her, makes her feel a bit envious. There was nothing like that twenty years ago.'

Juliet nodded. She tried to imagine what it would be like to have no chance of a baby of one's own. She couldn't imagine it. She didn't want babies for some years yet; she wasn't ready for them. Of course, if she found the right man, and she loved him —— Now why did she suddenly think of David Kent? Wasn't it Nigel she liked? Nigel. He was getting very intense about her, and she was worried. Shouldn't she be pleased?

Douglas opened the front door. 'We'll be back about half-past ten. Put some flowers about the place. She likes flowers.'

Juliet recalled her mother's suggestion yesterday. Flowers. She'd find some in the garden, after she'd had breakfast. But her mouth was dry with tension, and she could only manage orange juice and coffee. And when she went into the garden all she could see were some fading lupins and irises, not enough to fill one vase. Anyway, Irene always complained about the way lupins shed their petals all over the polished table. The columbines seemed to have disappeared, and the delphiniums weren't ready yet.

Juliet went back into the house and fetched her purse. She'd just have to go and buy some. It hadn't rained,

and her bicycle was still where she'd left it — again — by
the fence. It was warm and sunny, and for a brief time,
as she cycled along to the nearest shops, she almost
forgot what was to come that day.

Yonder, the town, had grown enormously during the
last twenty years. There was still the original village, of
course, now known as Old Yonder, and barely heard of
by outsiders until the building of Riverside General
Hospital on the outskirts. Most of Yonder was new,
housing estates, schools, shops, small businesses and
offices, and not entirely approved of by the original
residents of the village. But progress had to come, they
said, shaking their heads.

Irene and Douglas Avery had moved to Deerhurst
Road right at the beginning of the expansion, just after
Juliet's birth. Irene had fully expected that Douglas's
move to a new branch would lead to promotion, but it
hadn't happened. These days she said little about it.

The nearest flower shop was not far; it was called
Rose's Garden and stood between a rather nice, old-
fashioned type of coffee shop, called Memories, and a
shop that sold reject china. Juliet stood her bicycle
against the wall and locked it before going inside.

The interior of the shop was rather dim, and smelled,
naturally, of flowers and damp moss. There was just
one customer being served, a tall man in a chunky
cream pullover. He was waiting while his vivid red roses
were wrapped in the distinctive lilac and silver paper.
Juliet pottered around, touching one flower, smelling
another, and finally deciding on some assorted carnations and some deep red pyrethrums. She wished the
man would hurry up; he didn't seem to be objecting to
the way the young assistant was dragging out the
transaction. But finally the cash register clunked shut.

'Thank you very much, sir, and I do hope everything
goes well.'

'Thank you for your kind regards.' Juliet looked up
sharply from a display of pot plants, and was disconcerted by the rush of colour to her cheeks. She hadn't
recognised him from the back, and now she stared at

him in surprise. Dr Kent, as he turned and saw her, seemed to be as surprised as she was.

'Well, well, well, fancy seeing you here,' he said in his velvety voice. The assistant stared at them curiously. 'You look quite different with your clothes on,' he went on, to Juliet's acute embarrassment. 'Well, you know what I mean—out of uniform.' He grinned mischievously at the florist.

Juliet found her voice. 'I didn't expect to find you here either,' she said spiritedly. 'I've come for flowers for my mother.' She looked pointedly at his red roses, and he caught the glance.

'Someone's birthday,' he said shortly. 'I thought your mother was being discharged today?'

'She is. I want to make the house look nice for her.'

'Ah, the feminine touch. Don't let me keep you. You have a day off?'

'Just a morning.'

'Same here. Well, I expect we shall meet again on Melrose. I'm looking forward to it. I want to know——' he lowered his voice intimately '—everything.' A little quiver ran through her. Then he strode out of the shop. The florist stared after him.

'Some people have all the luck,' she said, shrugging. 'Can I help you?'

Juliet bought the flowers, and fixed them to the carrier on her bicycle. All the way home she found her mind turning to the red roses, and the person whose birthday it was. A girlfriend? The roses had been definitely red. Then she scolded herself for getting carried away, when she should be preparing how best to approach her mother over the subject of Elaine.

She had just finished arranging the flowers when Irene and Douglas returned, followed by an excited Domino. Irene looked a little pale, and Douglas helped her to a chair near the fire. Juliet kissed her and asked her how she was.

'A bit tired, but the doctor said that was to be expected for a day or two. I'm very relieved there was nothing seriously wrong.' Irene glanced around the room. 'The flowers are very nice.'

Juliet had put on the percolator earlier. Now she fetched in the tray, and they all sat down. She had butterflies inside, nerving herself for the questions she was about to ask.

'It wasn't as bad as you expected, was it?' she said brightly.

'Oh, no, not nearly as bad. I suppose I was remembering all those tests I had so long ago, all those nasty little operations——' Irene broke off, looking intently into her cup of coffee, as if it were to blame.

Juliet took a quick breath. 'Over twenty years ago, you mean.'

Irene nodded, and sipped her coffee. 'Yes, but I try not to think of those days. I'd rather forget——'

'It must have been terrible for you when they told you there was nothing more they could do,' Juliet said quickly. 'And it must be painful for you, even now, when all the papers and magazines are full of stories about test-tube babies and IVF and surrogate mothers and such.'

Irene shrugged. 'I put it to the back of my mind.'

'And yet you were luckier than some, I suppose,' Juliet hurried on. 'You were almost too old to adopt, weren't you, so when Elaine had her baby and was willing to let you have it, it must have seemed——'

Red spots of colour burned in Irene's pale cheeks. Juliet wondered if she was going about it too forcefully, but she had to know!

'Elaine died!' Irene insisted. 'It wasn't a question of her being willing. It was Malcolm—he couldn't cope. But you knew all this before, Juliet; why are you raking it up now?'

Juliet put down her coffee and went to sit next to her mother on the sofa. She put a hand on her arm.

'Mum, I hate to do this, I really do, but I have to know the truth.'

Her mother stiffened. 'What are you talking about?'

She turned to look for Douglas's support, but he had taken his coffee and retreated with the dog.

'I'm talking about Elaine. Mum,' Juliet looked into her mother's face, 'I was in the ward on Tuesday morning while the doctor was talking to you. I didn't intend to eavesdrop, I thought he'd gone and forgotten to pull back the curtains. And I heard him read from your notes that you were an only child, with no brothers or sisters. I couldn't believe what I was hearing, so I asked Dad.'

Irene said nothing. Suddenly she looked much older than her fifty-two years. Juliet felt a twinge of guilt at causing her pain.

'Elaine wasn't your sister, was she, Mum?' asked Juliet softly.

'She *was* your mother!'

Juliet nodded. 'I know. I want you to tell me all about her.'

Irene sighed and put down her cup. 'This is the day I always dreaded might arrive. At first I thought Elaine might suddenly turn up, then, as the years passed, I began to feel safe. It was my own fault, I suppose, for not telling you the whole truth, but I did it for your sake, because I loved you so much!'

Juliet felt the prick of tears behind her eyelids. Irene had never been demonstrative; Juliet couldn't recall her ever saying she loved her. It was ironic that, now she was preparing to share her daughter, she could reveal her feelings.

'I know,' she said. 'I'm really trying to understand, but it's been quite a shock to me. I always thought — Never mind. Go on, tell me.'

The clock in the hall chimed the hour. In the kitchen, Douglas spoke in a low voice to Domino, and the dog whined.

'I met Elaine in the hospital Outpatients. I was waiting to hear the results of the final tests, and she was waiting — well, for someone like me, I suppose. She had a huge holdall with her — I should have been suspicious, but I wasn't, I was too wrapped up in my own problems. The baby—you—was only ten days old. So tiny, so perfect, and all that dark hair! I was so envious of Elaine.'

Irene gave a wry smile and looked at Juliet. Juliet felt she was seeing another side to her mother, sensitive, vulnerable, and brave.

'She said your name was Juliet, but you hadn't been registered yet. She was planning to go the next day. She said she was a widow, her husband, Malcolm, had died at the beginning of her pregnancy. She didn't tell me how, and I didn't like to ask her—we'd only just met! I tried to feel sorry for her, but all I could feel was envy. She had the one thing I had always wanted. She watched me go in to the doctor. She even crossed her fingers for me. I couldn't help but like her.'

'She sounds nice,' said Juliet, her throat hurting.

'She was nice—sort of naïve and innocent. I know that sounds silly, when she had a baby——'

'Do I look like her?'

'Yes, you do. She had black hair, too, a sort of spiky cut, but that was the fashion then. Her eyes—no, I think they were a deep grey, not as blue as yours. Same sort of features, though, same build. She wasn't very tall—tiny, really. She looked too young to be a mother. She said she was twenty. Elaine Webb, she said her name was. Mrs Elaine Webb.'

She shifted in her chair, and grimaced slightly. Juliet waited.

'The news from the doctor was the worst. I'd wanted Doug to be with me, but he couldn't get the time off. I almost went to pieces in that room. It was like a nightmare, all my hopes dashed.' Irene twisted her hands together. 'Then, when I came out—and I must have looked dreadful—there she still was, the baby in one arm, scribbling madly on a sheet of paper with the other. I went to sit by her, I don't know why, because seeing that baby was twisting the knife tighter, but I did, and she put her arm around me while I told her.'

'I never knew it was like that,' murmured Juliet.

'She was so very young, yet she seemed to understand what it could be like, being denied the one thing you wanted. I was upset, so I held the baby while she fetched me a cup of tea. She waited while I drank it. And all I could think of was the way that baby had felt in my arms, and inside I was hating God for doing this to me.'

'Oh, Mum!'

Irene forced a smile. 'Elaine said she had to go for a blood test. Looking back, it should have sounded strange, after waiting all that time in the gynae clinic, and not even seeing a doctor. But I wasn't thinking straight. She asked me if I'd hold the baby while she went, as it might be cumbersome taking the bag and all. I was only too pleased.'

Juliet had a hunch what was coming next. 'She didn't come back?'

'She never came back,' said Irene. 'I sat there for ages, waiting, talking to the baby. I wouldn't have known what to do if you'd cried, but you didn't. You were so good. An hour went by, but I didn't really notice. I was making the most of this opportunity. I didn't care how I felt after you'd gone. I was trying to pretend you were mine.'

'Did no one else notice you were still there?'

'Oh, yes, a nurse came across; she'd remembered I'd already seen the doctor. I suppose it was then I began to realise something was wrong. I had to think quickly. So I said I was waiting for my sister, Mrs Webb. I asked where the blood tests were done — of course, I already knew — she told me. I staggered along with the baby and the heavy bag, and, of course, Elaine wasn't there. She hadn't been. Someone complimented me on my beautiful baby, and I suppose that was when the idea came into my head. I went and ordered a taxi, and I took you home.'

Irene gave a big sigh, of relief, Juliet supposed. She had to feel relieved after all these years.

'What did Dad say?'

'He was horrified; wanted me to take the baby to the

police. But how could I? A police cell, when you were
so warm and cosy in our house? We had plenty of room
for you, even a small nursery upstairs——' Irene broke
off and blew her nose.

'Didn't you tell anyone?' Juliet was horrified.

'Not straight away. You see, I'd given Elaine our
address—she wanted to keep in touch. So she knew
where we lived, and I expected her to turn up and claim
you.' Irene shifted in her chair. 'No, that's not true. I
told your father she'd turn up, but no, I never really
expected her to, not then. She'd planned it, I could see
that. That holdall, it held everything a baby could
need—food, clothes, nappies.'

'I'm surprised she didn't put in a gold locket or
something, or a precious necklace that could be traced
back to royalty, or the aristocracy, or the Sultan of
Kashmir, or the Pope.'

Juliet even surprised herself at the bitter words spill-
ing over. Irene looked hurt.

'No, Juliet,' she said softly, 'it was nothing like that. I
don't even know whether anything she told me was the
truth. Perhaps she wasn't a widow. Perhaps the father
had left her to face it alone, I don't know. But it
certainly wasn't the Oliver Twist story over again.
There wasn't a locket—but she left a letter.'

Juliet leaned forward in her chair. 'What did it say?'

'It said she hated having to give you up, she'd hoped
to keep you, but this way you'd have more than she
could ever give you, and she knew you'd be loved, even
as much as she loved you. Something like that. I can't
remember the exact words.'

'She must have planned it before she went to the
hospital.'

'I think she had some idea, that's why she chose the
gynae clinic. But I don't think that letter was written
until she'd decided who to leave the baby with. It said
something about finding the right mother for you,
knowing you'd be all right, and she could rest contented.
I think she wrote it while I was talking to the doctor,

crying my eyes out. She hid it inside a pile of nappies, so I didn't find it straight away.'

'Didn't the police look for clues to her identity?'

'They knew her identity: Elaine Webb. Yes, they looked in the bag, but I'd put all the stuff away by then, and they found nothing. It was very strange, almost as if it had been timed to happen, but the social worker came and was set to take you away. I was bathing you, and I fetched a clean nappy, and when I unfolded it the letter dropped out, and we read it.'

'And she let you keep me?'

'It was meant to be temporary, but Elaine wanted me to have you, and I think that influenced the social worker. She looked at your nursery, and all the things you'd got, and said you could stay until they'd found suitable adoptive parents. Well, the time went on, and eventually they approved us as adoptive parents, and that was that. We could keep you.'

'It makes me sound like a parcel that got sent to the wrong address.'

'Oh, Juliet, please don't think like that! Elaine could have left you on a doorstep, wrapped in a tea-towel. She loved you, Juliet, wanted the best family for you, one she'd chosen herself.'

'Why did you tell me Elaine was your sister?'

'I don't know. I thought it was a good idea at the time. I thought, if you knew you'd been abandoned, it might make you feel insecure, and I felt there was no need for you to know that.'

'Mum, don't you see? It wouldn't have mattered. By the time you told me I was adopted, I wouldn't really have cared who my real mother was. You were my mother, as far as I was concerned. A sister, a stranger — it wouldn't have mattered. I had you and Dad, and you were all I needed.'

Irene nodded slowly. 'Yes, I can see that now. Well, now you know it all. You've still got us, all you need, so now you can forget all about it. Blame me for having it sprung on you like this. I didn't mean it to happen this way.'

Juliet looked uncertain. 'I suppose that would be the easiest thing to do, for you and Dad. If you'd told me all those years ago, I would have grown up with the idea of another mother, perhaps miles away, perhaps just around the corner. But now—perhaps needing just you and Dad isn't enough. Elaine is my flesh and blood. She isn't dead—well, I hope she isn't—and I can't just put her out of my mind. Mum—I want to find her.'

CHAPTER FOUR

SISTER ROBINSON put down the phone in the office as Juliet and the junior nurse, Frankie Elmore, arrived to start their late shifts.

'Should be a nice busy afternoon for you girls,' she said cheerfully. 'That was Casualty. A young girl with agranulocytosis is coming in to Room C.'

'What's that?' asked Frankie. 'Agranu—something.'

'I think——' began Juliet hesitantly. 'Isn't it something to do with the white blood cells, the immune system?'

Sister smiled. 'You're quite right. This girl is seventeen, apparently homeless, living rough, presenting with an ulcerated throat and severe anaemia. Her name is Hayley Burton. And because of the grave risk from infection, she's to be barrier nursed in isolation.'

'Poor kid,' murmured Frankie, from her superior age of eighteen.

'At the moment no visitors, until her condition has been fully assessed. A boyfriend came with her, rather unkempt, so keep him out for the time being at least. I want you to get the room ready, with a supply of masks and gloves, and gowns just inside the door. Perhaps if you'd do that, Nurse Elmore, and Nurse Avery can get the four-hourly observations done before visitors.'

Juliet always liked doing temperatures and blood-pressures. It gave her a chance to talk to the patients. She went into Bobbie Cole's room first, as quietly as possible. Bobbie was resting. A magazine lay opened on the bed.

'How are the legs?' asked Juliet, as she wrapped the cuff around her arm.

'Still can't feel them. I got a bit worried yesterday, but one of the top nerve doctors came today, and he reassured me a lot—said I could be a lot worse, in

Intensive Care. And he seems to think I may not get any worse, but we shan't know for a couple of weeks.'

'That's wonderful news,' said Juliet, and took her temperature. 'Just think if it had been polio or something like that.'

'I can tell you,' said Bobbie, as Juliet recorded her findings, 'I shall treat my legs with a lot more respect after this!'

Juliet laughed, and went across to Room F, where Donna Hazell was sitting by the window reading a book. She was a pretty girl, with expressive dark grey eyes, and dark brown hair in a long bob. Seated, she appeared smaller than usual, and more fragile.

'Like it?' she asked, as Juliet entered the room, and patted her hair.

'Your new wig? It's great! Like your own hair?'

'A perfect match! And even better — I may be going home next week.'

'Even better! Now ssh.' Juliet popped the thermometer under Donna's tongue. Donna seemed very anxious to impart more news, so Juliet quickly recorded the temperature.

'I'm almost in remission, but that doesn't mean I'm cured. So, in case it does come back, my whole family are going to be tissue-typed.'

'I heard they were planning a bone-marrow transplant.'

'I don't suppose either of my parents will be suitable, they aren't usually. But I've got two brothers, so I'm sure one of them will be a match.'

'Younger than you?'

'Jamie's just doing A levels, Gary's fifteen, and he wants to be a train driver. Still!'

They both laughed, and Juliet felt a bond of affection growing for the other girl. Not just because she was the same age, but because she had such a dreadful illness, just when she should be enjoying life.

'You're training to be a teacher, aren't you?' she asked.

Donna nodded. 'I shall probably have to do this year

again, but it can't be helped. Chris says I could do it with my eyes shut, but he's biased.' She laughed, and went a bit pink.

'Who's Chris?' asked Juliet.

'He's a teacher I met on teaching practice. He's a bit older than me, his wife died, but he's really nice, and he's promised to keep in touch. I really like him.' She fiddled with the book, one by Margaret Atwood. 'I haven't told anyone else about him. I suppose I find it easy to talk to you.'

'It's our secret,' promised Juliet, and went to finish the observations.

She was thinking about Donna later, as she walked down the ward to see if the new patient had arrived. Two brothers — lucky girl. It wasn't the first time Juliet had wished she weren't an only child. But no use blaming anyone, least of all her mother. And then she found herself thinking about Elaine. She'd be forty now, if she'd told Irene the truth. She'd probably be married, with other children. My half-brothers and sisters, thought Juliet. I wonder if she thinks of me?

She was jolted out of her reverie by the noisy opening of the ward doors, and the rattling of a trolley being pushed between them. Sister came out of her office and took charge, and, with Juliet's help, they manoeuvred the girl on to the bed in Room C.

Hayley Burton was thin and very pale, with small sores around her mouth and nose, greasy fair hair that hadn't been washed in weeks, and dark-shadowed pale blue eyes. She wore grubby jeans, torn at the knees, and an unironed acrylic sweater which had seen better days. As the porters wheeled the trolley away, the girl opened her eyes and stared at Juliet with pure hatred. Juliet was taken aback.

'Poor kid,' murmured Sister. 'Let's get these things off her, shall we? Then we can get her washed.'

Hayley muttered epithets all the while they were working, but she was too ill to protest strongly. Soon she was fresh and clean, washed with a bar of perfumed soap one of the women had left behind, and looking virginal in a white cotton gown. With her long hair combed, she looked reasonably presentable.

'Where's Vince?' she demanded suddenly. 'I want Vince.'

'Is he your boyfriend?'

'Yeah. He brought me here—just for some medicine, he said. Said I wouldn't have to stay in. You just can't believe anybody, can you?'

'You came in a car?'

'Nah, Ron's van. He nicked some petrol.'

Sister and Juliet exchanged glances. 'Where are your parents?' asked Sister.

'Mum's in Gloucester, dunno where me dad is. He was in Tewkesbury. Don't really care. I'm better on me own.'

'How can you say——?' Juliet began, but Sister stopped her.

'I think we'll talk about that when you're feeling better,' she said gently. 'But as you're a minor, we really do need to contact one of your parents.'

'Will they have to come and see me?' Juliet detected fear in the girl's voice.

'Not unless you want them to,' said Sister.

'Well, I don't. If you promise not to tell them where I am I'll give you my mum's address. But I don't want my stepdad anywhere near me! Not even in the same hospital!'

'I think we can promise that,' said Sister. 'Now, the doctor will be coming soon——'

'I've just been seen half a dozen. They thought I was something the cat brought in.'

'I'm sorry you feel like that, Hayley. Nurse Avery, will you stay? Ah, here he is now.'

Juliet turned as David Kent strode into the room, tying a mask over his face, so that all she could see was his soft brown eyes. His gaze went straight to the girl in the bed.

'So you're Hayley. And what have you been up to?'

A look of panic crossed her face, darkening her pale eyes. 'Don't you start!' she retorted. 'I've had enough

with that lot downstairs, going on at me as if I'm
something less than bacteria!'

Juliet was shocked by the girl's vehemence. David
Kent paused in his approach. He glanced at Juliet
before gently taking the girl's thin wrist.

'I'm sorry if they upset you, but they were obviously
wondering, as I am, how such an obviously intelligent
girl allowed herself to get into such a state.'

'Don't patronise me! I'm just ill, that's all, got a sore
throat. And that's all you've got to sort out, nothing
else! Just leave me to live my life as I want.'

She pushed herself down in the bed, as if trying to
escape accusing glances.

'You're quite right,' David agreed, his fingers still on
her wrist. Sister smiled and left the room.

It was amazing the way David soon managed to
charm the girl into co-operating with him. He examined
her thoroughly, talking softly all the while, as Juliet
helped by supporting the girl. Her skin was hot. Finally
it was over, and David started to write up the notes. He
had taken specimens of blood and throat swabs, and
these waited on the cupboard to go to the laboratory.

Hayley lay silently in the bed, her gaze travelling
between David and Juliet, and the chart, trying to see
what he was writing.

'What you got masks on for?' she asked suddenly.
'It's frightening.'

'I'm sorry,' said David, 'but your throat condition
means you could become seriously ill if you came into
contact with the wrong sort of germs. I'm a bit concerned about those sores around your mouth. How long
have you had them?'

Hayley touched the sores on her face. 'Not long.
They're nothing.'

David finished writing. 'I expect you're wondering
what you've got. Well, we've got a good idea, but the
blood tests will tell us more. We believe you've got a
severe form of anaemia.'

'Can't I have some iron tablets?'

'It's not as simple as that. Are you sure you haven't been

taking any drugs, tablets, medicines of any sort ——' she
shook her head violently, but refused to meet his gaze
'— or any antibiotics during the last six months?'

'No — nothing! I've had nothing. I'm very healthy.'

'Did you really expect to stay healthy, living rough as
you have been doing, not eating enough, I expect ——'

'Leave me alone! We managed all right. I'm old
enough to look after myself. And I've got Vince. He's
twenty-two, and he'd do anything for me, get me
anything I want. We've got this squat, see, in
Gloucester — well, we did have it, but the council took it
back — but Vince has got friends in Tewkesbury, they'll
know about places, and that's where we were going
when I fell ill.'

Talking had exhausted her, and she lay back, breathing rapidly.

'When did you last see your mother?' asked David
gently. Juliet heard the concern in his voice, and her
heart contracted.

'A year ago. When I left home.'

'As soon as you left school,' said David flatly.

'If you thought I was going to stay there once I was
old enough to leave, with my stepdad still there — always
going on at me, touching me, pawing me, trying it
on —— What do you expect?'

Juliet held her breath. Poor kid! she was thinking.

'Didn't want to leave my mum, but she wasn't much
use to me — he treats her like dirt, knocks her about. She
couldn't protect me, could she? I had to think of myself,
didn't I?' Hayley glared defiantly at them. 'He'd have
started on me. Hit me — and worse.'

The room seemed heavy and quiet. Juliet couldn't
hear any sound from the ward. Then a tea trolley
clattered in the distance, and the tension broke.

David took Hayley's hand in his, and Juliet felt a
strange warmth steal through her, and a pang of some
emotion she didn't recognise.

'Hold tight, Hayley,' he said gently. 'You've had a
bad start, and you're not going to be over this illness in
a couple of days, but I'm sure you can beat it. And who

knows? Perhaps things will be better once you're over it.'

'Anaemia, you said? The blood? Oxygen and all that?'

'Yes, something like that. But not an ordinary anaemia. Don't worry, we'll sort it out.'

'You won't let them come here, will you?'

'Not even your mother? Don't you want to see your mother? She's bound to be very worried about you.'

'I only want to see Vince. Just Vince. Where is he?'

'I'll see what I can do.' David left the bedside, the file under his arm. Juliet tidied Hayley's bed, and gently pushed her hair from her face. Hayley stared at her, and a faint smile started. Then she looked away, as if ashamed to show her feelings. At least it hadn't been a look of animosity, as before, thought Juliet. David Kent seemed to be achieving near miracles.

Outside, David turned to her. 'Where is he? The boyfriend?'

'Sister wouldn't let him in. He's very scruffy, she said.'

'So was Hayley, I should imagine. She's been living with this guy for months, by all accounts, so she's probably immune to his germs by now. Make sure he washes his face and hands, then let him in, masked and gowned, of course. Tell him ten minutes, and no physical contact. It will be good for her psychological health to see him.'

'He's in the visitors' room. I'll tell him.'

Vince was standing at the window, looking out. He wore a long camelhair overcoat, Dr Marten's boots, and his sandy hair grew spikily down his neck. When he turned, Juliet wasn't surprised to see a straggly reddish beard. His eyes were bright blue. He shoved something into his pocket and came towards her.

'Where is she?' he asked aggressively. 'Is she coming out today?'

'You'll have to talk to the doctor. Hayley is very ill.' She explained the need for absolute cleanliness, showed him where he could wash, and told him about the masks and gowns.

He took off his coat reluctantly, and hung it over a chair. Juliet noticed he too had small spots around his nose and mouth, and an idea began to form.

'Ten minutes,' she told him, when he was ready to go into Room C. She went back to the visitors' room to open the window. It smelled stuffy. A small object lay on the floor near the chair where Vince had placed his coat, and she picked it up. A small plastic bag, rather sticky and smelling of chemicals.

David Kent was in the office, talking to Sister, when Juliet knocked and entered. Sister frowned.

'Something wrong, Nurse Avery? Did you make sure that undesirable young man cleaned himself up before he saw Hayley?'

'Yes, Sister. I — I found this on the floor after he'd left the visitors' room.' She held it out. 'I thought it might be significant to Hayley's illness.'

David took it, and their fingers brushed briefly.

'What is it?' asked Sister.

'Evidence of glue-sniffing, if I'm not mistaken,' said David, laying it on the desk. 'You were very wise to bring it to me, Nurse Avery.' His eyes met hers briefly, before looking away. Juliet flushed at his praise.

'Of course!' said Sister. 'Solvent abuse. Aplastic anaemia.'

'It's one of the causes,' David agreed. 'It had crossed my mind — the sores around her nose. But getting her to admit it would have been the problem. Tell the young man I want to see him before he leaves, Nurse Avery. Don't tell him what you've found, tell him I want to discuss Hayley's illness.'

'And then help Staff with the drugs,' said Sister. 'And then go to tea.'

'Yes, Sister.' Sister turned away, and, as she reached the door, David Kent gave Juliet a broad, conspiratorial wink that sent a little shiver through her.

Evening on the ward was much quieter. Sister was off duty, and Staff Nurse Target and Frankie Elmore both went to first supper, leaving Juliet in charge. Staff Nurse

Target needed to be back for visiting hour, as there were always some visitors asking questions.

It was while they were away, and the auxiliary helping the patients to make themselves presentable, that David returned. He came in and sat next to Juliet, watching her as she checked fluid-balance sheets. She felt very conscious of his presence, and it was with relief that she completed her task and sat back in the chair. She felt herself redden slightly under his gaze.

'Well?' he asked.

'Well, what?'

'You promised to tell me all about it. You haven't gone back on your promise, have you? I've been agog all afternoon, waiting for the next episode in your mystery story.'

Realisation dawned. For the past few hours she had been too busy to think of her own problem.

'I'd almost forgotten,' she admitted. 'I've been doing as you suggested the other day—putting the patients first.' She gave him a roguish glance.

'Oh, come on, don't leave me in suspense. Did you talk to them?'

'I spoke to my father last night, and he confirmed what I suspected. And this morning I had a long talk with my mother.'

'And Elaine wasn't her sister,' said David.

'Fancy you remembering her name,' said Juliet lightly.

'Nothing to be amazed about. I'm very interested.'

An interesting case study, thought Juliet—I suppose that's all it is to him. And why should it be otherwise?

'Yes, you're quite right.' And she told him all that Irene had told her that morning. When she finished David let out a low whistle.

'It's almost too fantastic to be true.'

'It may be fantastic,' Juliet agreed, 'but it's the truth. It really happened. It's happening all the time.'

'Not all the time,' put in David. 'Most babies are adopted in a routine fashion, not dumped on complete strangers. Yet I have to admit Elaine had really thought it out. What I don't understand is, if she wanted you to be adopted from the start, why didn't she go through the usual channels?'

'She wanted to choose the family herself,' suggested Juliet, who hadn't looked at it that way.

'It doesn't usually work out like that. She could have chosen a quite unsuitable family for you, and the social workers would have taken you away. As it was, she was fortunate your mother was accepted by the social worker. No, I think Elaine meant to keep you, then something happened and she was forced to give you up.'

'Do you think she ever knew her plan had worked? I mean, that my parents were allowed to keep me?'

'Impossible to say. She could have watched the papers, I suppose, could even have stayed in the area and watched you grow up. Had you thought of that?'

Juliet was shocked. It had never occurred to her that Elaine would have been brave enough to do that. She shook her head.

'So if I put an advertisement in the paper, asking her to get in touch, you think she might?'

David shrugged. Then he turned to her, a concentrated look on his face. His eyes met hers with a strange sort of intensity. 'You want to find her?' he asked.

'Wouldn't you? Of course I want to find her.'

'Is your mother aware of how you feel?'

'I told her, yes. I don't know whether she took me seriously. She accepted that it had been a shock to me, and she understood that I was feeling upset.'

'Are you shocked? Upset?' He was still watching her with that professional expression on his face. She looked away and fiddled with some pathology reports on the desk.

'Not now,' she admitted. 'I was, yes, but I'm growing used to the idea now. Although it is traumatic, having one's life turned upside-down like this, discovering I'm not the person I used to be. Having no roots, I suppose — it would upset anyone.'

'And disappointment in your parents, too, for keeping it from you.'

'Anger, I think. I did feel angry. But once she'd explained I felt much calmer. She did it for love, and how can I be angry with that?' To her amazement she felt tears pricking her eyelids. 'It's because she loves me so much that I just can't hurt her. If it's too painful for her to accept that I want to look for Elaine, then I shan't.'

'You'd do that?' David seemed surprised.

'Of course. She's my mother, not Elaine. Elaine is my roots, my past, but my mother is my life. It sounds dramatic, but you know what I mean.'

David nodded. 'Yes, I do. And I think you're quite amazing. You sound so pragmatic, yet I can imagine just how you're feeling.'

It was Juliet's turn to be surprised. She looked up to meet his gaze, and was immediately aware of the sudden tension in the air, a cross-current of electricity that seemed to flow between them. It almost took her breath away. She knew her hands were trembling as she fiddled with a pen on the desk.

'I don't see how——' she began, her voice catching in her throat. She swallowed, and tapped the pen nervously on the pile of papers. David's hand reached out and covered hers. It was warm and comforting.

'I can see it upsets you,' he said softly, and she was afraid to look at him, afraid to see again what she imagined she'd seen in his eyes. 'And I think you're more worried than you realise.'

Oh, yes, thought Juliet, I'm worried, but not for the reason you think. 'I'm all right,' she mumbled, her hand still imprisoned beneath his strong one.

'Would you like me to help you find Elaine?' He sat back, releasing her hand. She could still feel the pressure of his fingers. She looked up at him.

'Do you know how?'

'Well, of course, you can go through the usual channels, wait for your original birth certificate to arrive, see a counsellor from the adoption agency——'

'That might be difficult.'

'You can't wait that long?'

'My birth certificate won't tell me anything. Elaine didn't register my birth before she gave me to Mum, and no one seemed to know anything about her, or where she was from. She was never found. I could ask my mother to try to remember more than she's told me, but it's a long shot.'

'Not to worry,' said David cheerfully. 'We'll just have to play it by ear. I've done it before.'

'You've done this sort of thing before?'

He nodded. His brown eyes were suddenly sombre and sad. 'I know someone else who was adopted. I helped her trace her natural mother, that's all. I'm not even sure I should —— But never mind.'

He stood up quickly, as though the subject pained him. Juliet wondered why he was willing to do it all again. Perhaps he'd fallen in love with the girl. Perhaps it hadn't turned out well, and he'd been blamed. But he'd traced the mother, he'd said so, so it couldn't be that.

Perhaps, thought Juliet, her heart thudding against her ribs, perhaps if he helps me he thinks he might fall in love with me too. Perhaps he's regretting his impulsive offer. Yet I wasn't imagining it, I did see something in his expression —— Her shoulders slumped. I suppose he's still in love with the other girl. Her vivid imagination created someone tall and slim, blonde and attractive. Someone like Sara Calvert.

'You're not listening.' David tugged a lock of black hair. She jumped up.

'Sorry, I was — miles away.'

For a moment a guarded expression crossed his face. Then he smiled, a professional smile that didn't reach his eyes.

'I said we've talked enough, and I'd better go and see Hayley Burton.'

Just then, Staff Nurse Target returned from supper.

'Problems, Dr Kent?' she asked, her gaze taking in Juliet's anxious expression.

'Not really.' He refused to look at Juliet. 'I want to

have a talk with Hayley, get to the bottom of this glue-
sniffing business.'

'Be gentle with her,' said the staff nurse gruffly. 'She's
a nice kid.'

'I'm always gentle,' he said softly, and Juliet felt a
little quiver deep inside her. He left the room, and she
heard his shoes whisper their way down to Room C.

'You'd better go to supper, Nurse Avery,' said Wendy
Target briskly. 'Did you finish the charts?'

'Yes, Staff.' Juliet left the room, glancing towards
Room C before going towards the lift. But David Kent
was nowhere to be seen. And for a brief moment Juliet
envied Hayley Burton.

'Hi,' Penny Rogers greeted her, her voice barely audible
over the hum and clatter of the dining-room.

'Hello.' Juliet took her plate of lasagne and glass of
orange juice to Penny's table. There were no spaces
anywhere else.

'How do you like Melrose?' asked Penny, drinking
her coffee.

'It's nice. Some very interesting patients at the
moment.'

'Interesting cases, you mean?'

'Well, both, I suppose. I try to think of them as
people first.'

Penny surveyed her. 'Are the doctors interesting too?'

Unaccountably, a tide of colour crept up Juliet's neck
into her cheeks. She pretended to pick up a dropped
paper napkin.

'They seem all right,' she said non-committally. The
lasagne was dry.

'And David Kent? You must have met him by now,'
Penny insisted. Juliet wished she'd sat in some corner.

'Yes, I've met him a few times,' she admitted.

'Dishy, isn't he?'

'He's all right, I suppose.' Why was her heart behaving in this ridiculous fashion?

'He'll get snapped up quickly,' said Penny, leaning

back and enjoying Juliet's discomfiture. 'That's if it hasn't happened already.'

'W-what do you mean?'

'Yours truly saw him leaving the Olympus Theatre in Gloucester on Wednesday evening. With the staff nurse on Rainbow. And they seemed to be old friends.'

'You saw them?' It was a mistake to show an interest. Now it would be all round the hospital that Juliet Avery liked David Kent, and was probably jealous of the chidren's ward staff nurse.

'I'd been to the leisure centre, just across the road. Saw them clear as daylight. Quite attractive, Moira Charles, don't you think?'

'I suppose so,' said Juliet flatly. The staff nurse was slim and golden-haired. Not unlike Sara Calvert, and almost as pretty.

'You can imagine how good they looked together,' said Penny, smiling at Juliet. 'The dark and the fair.'

Juliet was stung to retort. 'I'm surprised you aren't making a bid for him yourself,' she said tartly.

Penny grinned. 'I would, but I'm spoken for. Anyway, it seems he likes blondes. Not much hope for you.'

Juliet pushed away her plate. 'I don't know what you're getting at. I hardly know him, and I'm spoken for too.'

'Of course! Nigel Westwood. Lots of dosh. You've done well there — more money than mere registrars.'

'You're incorrigible!' Juliet left the room, trying to ignore Penny's soft laughter that followed her.

CHAPTER FIVE

NEXT morning the ward was so hectic that Juliet was glad she had a half-day, and relieved that she could go to Nigel's party without having to persuade someone to change shifts with her.

Hayley Burton in Room C was feeling angry and tearful at being found out in the matter of the glue-sniffing. Vince had reluctantly admitted his part in it, but had tried to appear nonchalant about the risks he was taking. Hayley had been given a blood transfusion, and, after her initial protests, had accepted it, and lay against the pillows listening to pop music via the headphones.

Sister succeeded in contacting Hayley's mother, but the woman was strangely reluctant to become involved. Sister persuaded her to come and talk to her as soon as she was able.

'The police won't be involved, will they?' she said fearfully on the phone.

'As far as I know there's been no crime committed, not by Hayley, at least.'

'Has she said much about — us? Me — and her stepdad?'

'Very little. But I can talk better face to face. Just you — she doesn't want to see her stepfather.'

'Not surprising. But he's gone, anyway. At least, I went — I suppose I could tell Hayley that. Will you tell her? Then I might be able to come and see her.'

'Very well.'

Sister relayed the situation to the rest of the staff, to ensure their discretion. Then she went to tell Hayley. Juliet was there.

'Don't know why she's bothering,' muttered Hayley. 'She never lifted a finger to help me before. Still, if he's gone — perhaps she'd better come.'

With a smile of relief, Juliet left to continue observations.

Bobbie Cole was more cheerful, and chatted about her children, in particular her eldest child, a girl of eight named Sally, who wanted to be a ballerina.

'She takes her examinations soon,' she told Juliet. 'I hope I'm out of here by then.'

Juliet tried to reassure her that she wasn't any worse than yesterday, and that had to be a good sign. Then she went to see Donna Hazell.

The two girls had become firm friends; they seemed to have so much in common, apart from their age.

'They're coming for tissue-typing tomorrow.' Donna seemed quite excited about it. She laid down her *Cosmopolitan* magazine, open at fashions, loose flowing shirts in jewel colours. The sort of designs Juliet liked too.

'My mother's not too keen, I can't think why,' said Donna. 'I mean, she must realise this is the best chance for me. It's unlikely she'd be suitable as a donor, she could probably be only a half-match at best. But she doesn't seem to want even Jamie and Gary — oh, hello, David!'

Juliet glanced quickly at the girl as she folded up the stethoscope. David? David Kent? She turned to look at the registrar as he strode smiling into the room, and her bemused expression must have registered.

'And how's my favourite cousin?' he asked, sitting on the bed.

'Going home soon, I hope. What's the latest?'

'The latest results are very good. The chemotherapy's working well.' Donna leaned forward and kissed him on the cheek.

'Soon?' she asked, and tugged at his hair.

'Fairly soon. But it doesn't depend on me. I'm only an underling.'

'My favourite underling,' grinned Donna. 'Isn't he yours, Juliet?'

Juliet went pink as she agreed teasingly, 'Oh, of

course, my very favourite underling.' She turned to him. 'You're cousins?'

'Of a sort,' agreed David. 'Our mothers are cousins, so we're second cousins once removed. Something like that.'

'His grandmother is my great-aunt,' added Donna.

'Sounds very complicated,' remarked Juliet, as she wrote on the chart.

'Not really,' said David. He stood up. 'Are they all ready for the vampires tomorrow?'

Donna laughed. 'Who could resist a vampire like you?'

'I shall want whole armfuls. Tell them to have liver for lunch.'

'David, you are funny!' said Donna, then she became serious. 'I hope my rare blood-group won't cause problems.'

'Put it this way, Donna. If you have a rare blood-group, then the odds are in favour of one of your brothers having the same. But it isn't the group that's so important, it's the leucocyte antigen that matters, matching all the different factors.'

'I hope one of them matches,' said Donna. 'Or I shall be stuck, shan't I, if the leukaemia comes back?'

'Let's cross that bridge when we get to it,' said David. 'We've got other tricks up our sleeves, you know. I'll see you tomorrow.'

Juliet smiled at Donna and followed him from the room. Outside, he turned to her. 'Where are you going now?'

'Coffee break.'

'How are you getting on with your search?'

'I'm a bit stuck where to start. You know, Elaine didn't register my birth, and we're not really sure whether the facts she gave were absolutely true, so it's going to be a matter of checking all babies born on the same day in the same area, and I'm not sure whether the people at St Catherine's House can do that sort of thing. I may have to go and search myself.'

'Don't you know anything else about her that might

give you a lead? She must have talked to your mother for some time, she must have let something slip.'

Juliet shrugged. 'I shall have to nerve myself to ask her, but I'm not sure she's very keen on the idea. I really wish there was a short cut.'

'I'd like to help you.' He took her arm. 'Got a straight shift?'

Juliet's heart seemed to give a little flutter as she answered, 'Half-day. But I'm going out this evening — a party in Cheltenham.'

'Boyfriend?' Did she imagine the shadow that crossed his face? Of course. He liked Moira Charles. And probably Sara Calvert too. And who knows how many more? she told herself. He buys someone red roses. Why should he be interested in me? Anyway, I'm not blonde.

'Yes, a boyfriend,' she said.

'Ex-patient from Bassett?'

Colour flooded her cheeks. 'How did you know?'

He shrugged. 'The grapevine. If you make dates with patients, you have to expect everyone to know. It's not really very wise.'

'I don't see how you can say that. Patients are just ordinary people, after all. They don't have six arms and two heads.'

'It's not the patients I'm talking about. But you know what they say about patients falling in love with the nurses. They all do it, to some extent, and if they take it further it's never the same as they imagine it to be. Nurses out of uniform just aren't glamorous any more, and it can be quite disappointing.'

'Who says Nigel has fallen in love with me?' said Juliet lightly. 'And even if he has, I can't see that it's any concern of yours, Dr Kent.'

His brown eyes narrowed. 'Don't say I didn't warn you.' He turned to go, then turned back again. 'Wealthy, is he?'

Juliet's cheeks burned. 'That's nothing to do with it!'

'I thought he was. Pity. Juliet——' he came closer and looked intently into her eyes ' — do you really want to go to his party?'

Her mouth seemed suddenly dry as she said, 'I've promised, and I don't like breaking promises.'

'Never mind promises. Do you want to go?' His tone was urgent, almost as though her answer was important to him.

She hesitated, momentarily. 'Of course I do.'

His shoulders seemed to sag. 'He won't miss you.'

'How can you say that? You don't know him!'

'I suspect you don't know him very well either.' He grasped her arm again. 'I'm off duty tonight. I could take you out. I'm going to see ——'

'Then I'd have to lie to him! I won't do it!'

He loosed her arm and stood looking at her, a slight frown on his brow. Juliet couldn't help gazing at his eyelashes, so long and curling, and wondered what it would be like having a date with David Kent. For an instant she was tempted to give in to him, to say she'd forget the party. But it wasn't fair on Nigel. And who did David Kent think he was anyway, waltzing in like this, and telling her who she should choose for her friends?

'So you've made up your mind?' His quiet voice broke in on her thoughts.

She lifted her chin. 'Yes. I'm going to the party. Did you really think I'd break my promise?'

'No. No, I didn't.' His voice was flat and heavy. He turned to go, and, once again, changed his mind. 'Be careful,' he said curtly. 'Don't come running to me when you get hurt.'

He turned abruptly away, and she watched him go along the ward to the office, a strange feeling inside her. Get hurt? Why should Nigel hurt her? They were just friends, and he was fun to be with. They laughed a lot, they kissed a lot. Nothing serious yet, although she sensed their friendship was changing in a subtle sort of way. His caresses had grown more intense just lately, his lovemaking more insistent. She was beginning to sense his need for her, and pondered whether she was ready for this final stage in their relationship.

I'm too old-fashioned, she thought. Most girls

wouldn't hesitate over this sort of thing. And surely if I loved Nigel I wouldn't hesitate either. So perhaps I don't love him. If I did, surely I would know?

She walked through the ward, beset by sudden doubts about the party on that evening. She had no idea whether it was to be a large gathering, or just a few intimate friends. Lots to drink, Nigel had said, but that meant nothing. Meet my friends, he'd said. How many did he have? Juliet was getting a strong feeling that this party was going to change their relationship in some way, but she didn't know how.

I thought I was falling in love with him! she told herself as she went down to the dining-room. But now I'm not so sure. How can I tell? I've never been in love before. David Kent's good-natured face floated into her mind. She could almost hear his voice again. 'Don't come running to me when you get hurt.' Almost as if he knew her turmoil.

Yes, I should know if I were falling in love, she thought. I'm sure David Kent would know. I expect he has fallen in love. She thought of the red roses, and it made her feel quite empty inside.

When Juliet returned from coffee, she was immediately thrust into helping with the admission of a new patient. Her name was Gaynor Summers, she was young, black, and in her mid-twenties. She was also plump and very breathless.

'My doctor thinks it's rheumatoid arthritis,' she gasped, as Juliet and Jill Herbert helped her into bed, 'but I didn't think it could affect your chest like this. I thought I'd got pneumonia.' She tried to laugh. 'My uncle in Jamaica died from pneumonia.'

'You mustn't think things like that,' Juliet reassured her. 'Don't you worry, we'll soon find out what it is.'

Jill left for her coffee break, and Juliet filled in the basic charts.

'We're new to the area,' said Gaynor. 'I've just got a new job at the solicitors in Yonder. I'm a secretary. We

lived in Cheltenham before. My husband works in a
shoe shop. He's a manager now, in Tewkesbury.'

'Good for him.' Juliet slipped a thermometer under
her tongue, and chatted to her while she waited.

'We've been married just over a year,' said Gaynor,
'and we don't want to start a family just yet. I'm only
twenty-five, and we want a place of our own. We've got
a flat now, very nice, but we'd like a house in Yonder,
down by the river, but I expect they're more expensive.'
A coughing fit overtook her and Juliet handed her a
tissue.

'Funny sort of arthritis,' said Gaynor shakily, just as
the curtains opened and David Kent came to the
bedside. He didn't even glance at Juliet, but began the
examination and the questions.

Eventually it was finished, various tests organised,
and chest X-rays. And all the time David had spoken
only briefly to Juliet, to move Gaynor and help her with
her gown. Each request had been made briefly and
tersely, until Juliet began to feel quite miserable. She
couldn't help thinking that perhaps she had been the
cause of his bad mood. Yet what had she done to cause
it? Merely refused to break a promise.

'Organise routine urine tests, Nurse Avery,' he called
back as he left the cubicles.

'Yes, Dr Kent.' She tidied the bed.

'He seems nice,' said Gaynor. 'But he doesn't say
much. Is he a good doctor?'

'He's an excellent doctor.' It was the truth, after all.
Whatever had happened to upset him, he was an
excellent doctor. Juliet smiled at Gaynor and went to
fetch her a bedpan.

Juliet hoped to get some studying done that afternoon,
before going to Nigel's party. But she was still in a state
of turmoil as she put her bicycle away and entered the
house. Nigel — David. How was it men could make you
feel so confused?

Her mother was resting on the sofa, reading a magazine. The remains of a sandwich lunch were on the side table.

'How are you, Mum?' Juliet asked, putting down her bag.

'Better than yesterday. I'll be all right.'

'Taking your iron tablets? Remember the doctor said you were a little anaemic.'

'You don't have to bring the hospital home with you,' Irene reminded her. 'Of course I've taken my tablets. Have you had lunch?'

'I had something at the hospital.' Juliet started to take some books from her bag. Domino hurtled in from the garden, and she rubbed his silky head.

'What time's the party?' asked Irene.

'Nigel's coming at six.'

'At last we're going to meet him. What does he look like?'

'Fairish, tall, slim, quite nice-looking.'

'And his father's a publisher? Is it a big firm? Well known?'

'Spinney Publishing. You've probably heard of it.'

Irene gave a little squeal of delight. 'Heard of it? They do all those biographies of politicians and royalty. Oh, Juliet, you've done well there.'

Juliet answered irritably, 'Everyone seems to assume I go out with Nigel because his family's wealthy. It's not like that at all! He was the one who made the running in the first place, and I quite like him.'

'It is nice, though, his being rich. Does he work in the business?'

Juliet had to admit to herself that Nigel seemed to do very little work at all.

'Oh, yes,' she said to her mother.

'Studying?' asked Irene, glancing at the books on the table.

'I'd planned to.' She picked up *The Social Aspects of Illness*. It sounded boring.

'We've hardly spoken since yesterday morning,' said Irene, closing her magazine. 'I thought perhaps you were still mad at me.'

'Oh, Mum, of course I'm not mad at you. Not now.
But it has left me feeling rather — confused. I feel — sort
of rootless, if you know what I mean.'

Irene bit her lip. 'You still want to look for Elaine.'

'Yes, Mum, I do. It's not because I don't love you
and Dad, you know that. But I want to know my
origins, my beginnings. I didn't begin here, with you
and Dad, I began with an unknown woman called
Elaine, a girl really, and a father who isn't in New
Zealand after all, but who might be in the next street,
the next house. As Elaine could be.'

'It's unlikely,' said Irene. 'I'd recognise her.'

'Perhaps the next town, then. She could have married
again — that's if she ever married before ——'

'She said she was a widow. Malcolm, his name was.'

'But was it the truth? The truth would make it easier
for her to be found, and she never was found, was she?
So it's very likely she told you a few fibs. Even as
recently as the nineteen-seventies, being an umarried
mother carried a stigma.'

Irene shrugged. 'You could be right.'

Juliet leaned forward and took her mother's hand. 'I
shan't look for her if it's going to hurt you, I promise.'

'Juliet, you go ahead. You know that all I've ever
wanted is your happiness. If finding Elaine will make
you happy, you go ahead. I know you'd never hurt me.
I'm afraid I've hurt you, so perhaps wanting you to do
this will somehow make amends. Find Elaine, and the
best of luck.'

There was a short pause, during which Juliet felt as if
an incredible weight had lifted from her shoulders. She
studied her mother's tired face, seeming older than her
fifty-two years.

'Tell me how to find her, Mum,' she said softly. 'I
don't know enough about her. Can't you tell me more?'

'I've told you everything I can remember. It was a
long time ago.'

'But it was such a significant day in your life. You
must remember all the things you talked about at the
hospital, while you were waiting to see the doctor. That

was before she chose you, so she may have told you more than she intended.'

Irene passed a hand across her brow. 'I'll try. I'll try to go back to the beginning. I was already there and she came and sat by me. At that moment I wished she hadn't, because she'd got that tiny baby, and it was such an effort trying not to look.'

'How awful for you.'

'I had to listen when she started to talk. I had to look at you, and make noises at you. I didn't know how to talk to babies.' Irene gave a short laugh. 'Yes, she told me how you'd been born early, weeks early, how you were very small, but not small enough for special care. Just under six pounds, she said. You were like a doll. I couldn't stop looking at you once I'd seen you.'

Juliet felt a surge of love and warmth inside her. She didn't speak.

'She'd been at work, she said, when she went into labour. Helping with old people, she said. She was rushed to the nearest hospital. No—it wasn't a hospital—it was a maternity home, a nursing home. That's right, she said it was just like a big house, and there was only one midwife on duty, and there was another girl in labour. Yes, I remember that.'

'Didn't she say where she'd been working? Was it local?'

'Let me think.' Irene closed her eyes. 'Pershore—near Pershore. Barkton—Berkton—Birk—leigh! Birkleigh! That's it. Something House in Birkleigh. The nursing home. Why do I think of roses?'

Juliet sat on the edge of the chair, willing her mother to remember. 'Roses? Flowers? Plant? Lilies?'

'Thorns. Thorn House,' said her mother suddenly.

'Thorn House, Birkleigh,' Juliet repeated. 'It shouldn't be too difficult to find. I've been through Birkleigh; it's only a village.'

'If it's still there,' said her mother slowly. 'It's twenty years. Old houses get pulled down, or changed into something else. Don't build your hopes up, Juliet. You'll only get hurt.'

Just what David had said. Why did everyone think
she couldn't cope with hurt? She was twenty, adult. She
was prepared for hurt.

'I have to look, Mum.'

'I know. But do you seriously expect the same people
to be there after so long? They won't remember you.'

'There'll be records, Mum. There are always records.
Oh, Mum, I need all that luck you wished me. I'm
going to visit my birthplace!'

Juliet was too excited to study. She had to restrain the
urge to rush out and get the bus to Birkleigh, to find
Thorn House, to see where Elaine had been. She'd been
right, *The Social Aspects of Illness* was pretty boring, and
she was glad when it was time to get ready for Nigel's
party. Should she tell him all her latest news? Would he
be as interested as David Kent? Something made her
decide to wait until she knew more.

'What are you wearing for the party?' asked Irene, as
they cleared away the tea things.

'Haven't made up my mind. I thought my red.'

'The colour suits you.' Irene agreed. 'But the style —
it's a bit tarty.'

'Are you sure? Perhaps my midnight-blue, then. I
don't want to look tarty, do I? But the blue's a bit old-
fashioned.'

'Old-fashioned is nice. The old styles are all coming
back. I'm sure his parents will like it.'

'Well——' Juliet took a deep breath.

'His parents are going to be there, aren't they?'

'Actually, no. They're away for the weekend.'

'I see. While the cat's away —— Are you being wise?'

'What are you talking about? Parties aren't the same
with parents there — they do clip one's wings somewhat.
They never like the music, for a start.'

'Hmm. A disco, is it?'

'I don't know. But you don't have to worry about me.
I shall be perfectly all right.'

Her mother walked away, holding the sugar bowl. I
am right, I'm sure I am, thought Juliet. It's just a party,

and parties are all the same. And she knew Nigel quite well by now. Well enough?

She changed her mind and put on her black velvet skirt and a fairly new satin blouse in kingfisher-blue that matched her eyes. It had a scooped neckline and billowing sleeves gathered into the wrists. She had showered and washed her hair, dabbed on her favourite Anaïs Anaïs, and stood before the long mirror in her bedroom, criticising her reflection. Her black hair suited her elfin face, cut short. The word elfin brought David Kent to mind. Elfin. He had called her a leprechaun, thought she must have Irish blood in her. Her pulses quickened. She looked like Elaine. Was it possible, the Irish blood? Her brilliant blue eyes must have come from her father. Turquoise, like a Caribbean pool, one boyfriend had said. No one had called her a leprechaun before. She smiled at her reflection.

If only she could have been taller. Five feet six inches would be nice. David was tall. Being taller would make her look slimmer, although she was quite slender now. Sara Calvert was quite tall. And Moira Charles would be almost as tall as David in high heels.

I wonder what she wore for the theatre date with David? Juliet wondered. Something dark to emphasise her fair colouring? With a gesture of annoyance, she reached for a rope of jet beads and fastened it around her neck. It looked good. Nigel would approve. She glanced at her watch. Any minute now he would be arriving, and she'd promised her mother she'd let her meet him.

She felt a brief quiver of uncertainty. How would Nigel react when he saw their small semi-detached, in a row of identical houses? Would it make any difference to their relationship? If he liked her for herself, it shouldn't. And would her parents like him?

The doorbell rang as Juliet fastened her black sandals. She grabbed her black crocheted shawl and velvet evening bag, and hurried down the stairs to open the door. In the porch, Nigel lounged nonchalantly against the wall. He wore cream linen trousers and a pale yellow shirt that was definitely not off the peg. Juliet wondered if she were overdressed, but the admiring look he gave her dispelled that thought. He rested his hand on her shoulder and gave her a long kiss on the lips.

'You look good enough to eat,' he murmured.

'Why, don't you have enough food at your house?' she asked smartly.

He patted her on her bottom. 'It was meant to be a compliment.'

'Sorry. I thought you meant I looked like a side of beef. Come on in and meet my parents.'

He pulled a face. 'Is it compulsory?'

'They want to meet you, they've heard a lot about you.'

'That sounds ominous! What do they suspect I get up to with their precious little daughter?' He pulled her to him as soon as she'd closed the front door behind them. 'Of course, chance would be a fine thing — oh, yes, chance would be a fine thing indeed!' He started to nuzzle her neck, but Juliet pulled away.

'Not here,' she protested. 'Come on in.'

Irene smiled delightedly when Nigel bent and kissed her hand, murmuring something about 'older sisters'. Juliet cringed. Not that old chestnut!

'I can see where she gets her beauty,' he said, gazing at Irene.

Irene looked puzzled and glanced at Juliet. 'But didn't —?'

'And this is my father. This is Nigel,' Juliet interrupted quickly, as Douglas came in from the garden. Domino hurtled past him, tail wagging madly, looking up expectantly at the stranger. Nigel patted the dog's head absentmindedly, and turned to Douglas.

'Did I drag you away from your gardening?' he asked, and laughed. 'You should see the size of our garden!'

Douglas murmured something. He hadn't been gardening, but happened to be wearing his casual clothes. 'Drink, Nigel?' he asked, turning to the drinks cabinet. Juliet wondered if he'd re-stocked it for the occasion.

'Better not,' said Irene quickly. 'He's got to drive to Cheltenham.'

'Oh, a small one won't hurt,' said Nigel smoothly, settling himself comfortably in an armchair. 'Brandy and soda, if you've got it.'

Juliet began to feel anxious again. She couldn't help thinking about the Porsche and Nigel's fractured pelvis. Still, one drink — and he was used to alcohol, wasn't he? She sat on the sofa and smiled at him.

'Doesn't she look gorgeous tonight?' he remarked, taking his glass.

'Please, Nigel —— ' Juliet felt embarrassed.

'What's wrong, my pet?' He tossed back his drink as if it were lemonade. 'Don't you like compliments? I can see I shall have to watch you tonight.'

Juliet went pink. 'Could I have a drink, please, Dad?' she asked, to hide her discomfiture.

'Oh, dear, no time for that, I'm afraid,' said Nigel, getting up. 'You ladies take far too long over your drinks, and we have a long drive ahead of us.'

He makes it sound like a hundred miles instead of nine, Juliet thought, rising reluctantly. She had hoped he would stay for a chat with her parents, but he was making it very obvious that that wasn't part of his plan.

'Do come again,' said Irene, following them to the front door.

'You're very kind.' He smiled charmingly.

'Shall you be late, Juliet?' asked Douglas. 'I could come and pick you up if you like —— '

'Oh, no, Dad, that won't be necessary at all.'

'I shall bring her back myself,' promised Nigel, and Juliet's heart sank.

The door closed behind them, and they went down the short path. Beyond the front gate, two youths were admiring the scarlet Aston Martin sports car. They watched enviously as Nigel and Juliet settled themselves inside. Then they were off with a loud revving of the engine.

As they drove out of town, along the quiet roads to the country, it became clear to Juliet that the brandy and soda her father had given him hadn't been Nigel's first drink of the evening. For a start, he was driving far too fast, had only just swerved in time to avoid a cyclist, and was now desperately trying to overtake a pale blue Renault, when it was obvious there wasn't room, and the road ahead was too winding to see if it was clear.

She held her breath as the road widened slightly, and with a roar the Aston Martin shot forward, only just reaching the safety of the road ahead before a black saloon appeared around the corner.

'Bit of a close shave, that,' she murmured, glancing at him.

Nigel laughed. 'Not my fault. Couldn't get round that doddering old snail. That sort should be in wheelchairs, not cars.'

Juliet said nothing. Her view of the driver of the Renault, albeit only a back view, had shown her the thick dark hair of someone obviously quite young. She was relieved when Nigel had to slow down as they reached the outskirts of Cheltenham. He turned a corner into a wide road edged with large detached houses, then drove along a broad lane, at the end of which was a wide circular drive, and at the top an imposing Georgian house. Juliet drew in her breath as she gazed at it.

She had always imagined Nigel's home to be large, but this was immense! She never imagined publishers could be as wealthy as this! The house was square and wide, of cream stone, with an imposing entrance as large as their sitting-room at home, a white arched and mullioned doorway, and lots of high leaded windows. Juliet had only seen windows like these in stately homes. This reminded her of a stately home. To the left was a huge glass conservatory, where she imagined palms and chamber music evenings. And the lawns seemed to stretch into infinity

'Clemency Park,' said Nigel. 'Come on, meet my friends.'

Still a little numb from shock, Juliet followed him into a huge hall, all gilt objects, velvet hangings, mirrors and oil-paintings. The party seemed to be taking place in a room off at the right. She could hear laughter and talking and the chink of glasses. No music yet. She felt very vulnerable and awkward as she followed him into the room. Everyone turned to look at her.

'This is Julie,' Nigel announced, tossing her shawl on a chair. 'You've got to be nice to her, because she helped to save my life.'

Someone cheered, and there were ribald comments. With surprise, Juliet realised he was referring to his hospital episode, when she had nursed him for the last two weeks of his stay. But save his life? Never. Smiling shyly, she went forward to meet them.

At first Juliet thought it was going to be fun. Everyone was very friendly — although some of the male guests made the usual predictable comments about nurses and male patients, and Juliet smiled through gritted teeth. Nigel held her arm possessively, squeezing it at intervals, although she couldn't think why.

Someone had put on a record, slow, lazy music, and the couples on the floor weren't really dancing, merely clinging to each other like limpets, nuzzling each other's necks. Juliet felt rather embarrassed when Nigel did the same, holding her body against his, while his hands moved suggestively over her hips, his mouth seeking hers. She was relieved when the record ended.

'It's very warm in here,' she said. 'I think I'll go and get some fresh air.'

'It's raining,' he told her gleefully. 'But if you really don't like my kissing you in public, why don't we go upstairs, where it's more private? We shan't get disturbed——'

Juliet gazed at him in dismay. What sort of party was this? She recalled her mother's words, and her own reassurances.

'It's not very polite to leave your guests,' she pointed out.

'They won't even notice. What do you think they've come for? I'm beginning to think you're a spoilsport, Juliet. I'm disappointed in you.'

She was still searching for the right words to describe how she felt when he suddenly got up and went to meet more guests, and she didn't see him for a long time. It didn't matter; she was plied with drinks — most of which she disposed of when no one was looking — and received frequent requests to dance.

She refused. No one was dancing, just smooching, and she didn't make a habit of smooching with almost strangers.

Then she saw Nigel dancing with a well-rounded girl with yellow hair and pouting lips. She was responding to his smooching with alacrity. She must know Nigel well, thought Juliet, watching them and feeling excluded. Perhaps I'm a prude, she thought, her glance returning to them. The girl wore a low-cut red dress — not unlike mine at home, she mused — very high heels, and lots of glittering accessories. Nigel was embracing her tightly now, and kissing her ear.

She's enjoying it, thought Juliet. She doesn't care who's watching. And she was surprised to find she wasn't remotely jealous.

A girl who seemed much older than the others came to talk to her. She said her name was Liz, she was a friend of the family, and she had done some nursing once, a long time ago, but gave it up to get married. She was now divorced, and she sometimes regretted not finishing her training. She'd liked hospital life; it was real.

Juliet was grateful to find a kindred spirit among all these wealthy public-school-educated socialites. They talked for ages, making their drinks last, and no one came and bothered them at all. Liz had just announced that this conversation had convinced her, and she was going to get a hospital job of some sort, when Juliet suddenly remembered Nigel. She looked around her with alarm.

'Nigel will be wondering where I am,' she exclaimed.

'We're not hiding,' Liz pointed out. 'He can find you if he wants to. I must admit he's neglected you rather shamefully. But he's like that, I'm afraid. He's got a lot of growing up to do. He's fun, but totally irresponsible. But you don't need me to tell you that. You must know.'

Juliet, only half listening, gazed around the room.

The numbers had dwindled, and she wondered why so many had left already. There was no sign of Nigel anywhere.

'I'd better go and powder my nose,' she told Liz, getting up. 'Where's the bathroom?'

'There are three on the first floor. Just push a likely door and you'll find one.'

Juliet walked slowly up the wide, curving staircase. At the top was a long gallery, and corridors leading from each end. Shrugging, she turned down the right-hand one, looking for 'likely doors'. She could hear voices ahead, a girl squealing, a man laughing. A door burst open and a girl in green ran out, shrieking excitedly, chased by a man waving a wispy bra. The girl was dishevelled, her hair a mess, but she only laughed as he caught her and pulled her into another room.

They'd left the other door wide open, and as Juliet passed, she caught sight of a rumpled bed with blue sheets. The next door seemed to be a likely one, it was not quite closed, so she gently pushed it open — gently, just in case she was wrong, and it was a bedroom.

In the doorway she stopped dead. It was a bedroom, and it was occupied. She stepped back, horrified, but not before she'd seen the naked arms and legs, the bright yellow hair against the emerald green pillow, the broad naked back of the man. Nigel.

She pulled the door quickly behind her, and stood for a moment, breathing fast. She wished she hadn't seen that, but perhaps it was best that she had. She found a bathroom further along, and sat on the edge of the bath. She couldn't stay, that was obvious. Not for another minute could she stay.

Once she'd finished in the bathroom, she hurried downstairs to collect her shawl. Liz was nowhere to be seen. Juliet could have asked someone to find a phone for her, to get a taxi, but she was aware that she was trembling, near to tears, and she didn't want people to ask questions. She threw her shawl around her shoulders and hurried from the house.

Nigel had been right about the rain, but she didn't
hesitate. The drive was much longer than she remembered, and by the time she reached the lane, her sandals
had grit in them, and her hair was quite wet. There
weren't any street lamps in this deserted road. She
hadn't reached the houses yet. The rain was getting
heavier, and she felt frustrated and angry. How could
she ever have been taken in by Nigel Westwood?
Indignant tears trickled down her face. Rain trickled
down her neck. Why had she agreed to come to his
awful party?

Limping, sniffing, aware that the rain could have
ruined her best velvet skirt, she stumbled along, her
eyes peeled for a phone box. There wasn't one in sight.
Eventually the houses started, and the street lamps,
shining yellow on the wet pavements. And there, in the
distance, a phone box!

For a few yards now she had been aware of a car
cruising behind her. Her heart beat fast. It drew along-
side her, a pale blue Renault that seemed vaguely
familiar. She remembered: the snail who should be in a
wheelchair, according to Nigel. She walked faster, trying
to run, but the grit in her sandals rubbed her heels. If
she could just get to the phone box —— The car cruised
along at her speed. Juliet tried not to panic. The window
was wound down.

'What on earth are you doing, dressed like that in this
weather?'

David Kent's voice! She stopped. A little sob formed
in her throat.

'For God's sake get in, or you'll get pneumonia!'

CHAPTER SIX

THE passenger door was pushed open. Holding her wet shawl tightly around her, Juliet almost fell into the car. She shut the door, and the car started to move away along the quiet road. She stifled a sob, but a little gulp escaped. David glanced at her. 'Are you all right?'

'I'm fine, thank you. I'd have been all right. I was about to ring for a taxi.'

'Cost the earth this time of night. What happened to the rich boyfriend? What was he doing, letting you wander the streets half dressed in the rain?'

'He didn't know I'd left.'

'Did you have a row?'

'No.' They were travelling along the country lanes by now, and the hum of the engine was soothing. 'Honestly, I'd have been perfectly all right.' She tried to inject confidence into her voice, but it came out shaky and weak.

'Oh, sure.'

There was silence for a while. The tyres hissed on the wet roads. Juliet glanced at David's strong profile. He was angry with her, but she couldn't imagine why. She was angry with herself, but that was different.

'How are you going to explain your sodden state to your parents?'

'Oh, they'll probably have gone to bed.' The clock on the dashboard showed twelve-ten. How quickly the evening had gone. Until that last few minutes, when she'd stood in the doorway of the room and watched Nigel making love to another girl. Those moments had seemed to pass in slow motion.

'I hope for your sake they have. If my place wasn't so much further I'd suggest you go there to dry off.'

The suggestion was casually made, but Juliet couldn't

stop the tide of hot colour that welled up into her face.
She was glad it was dark, and he couldn't see it.

'You don't have to worry about me,' she said in a
small voice.

'It seems someone's got to worry about you, running
around without a coat in this weather.' He glanced at
her blue satin blouse. Juliet was suddenly aware of the
lowness of the neckline, and the way the rain had caused
it to cling to her figure. She pulled the damp shawl over
her shoulders. David smiled.

'What was wrong with the party?' he asked.

'I'd rather not talk about it, if you don't mind.'

'Hmm.'

Juliet knew that in the future any mention of
Cheltenham would make her see Nigel and that girl
with the yellow hair. She'd been quite prepared to give
him what Juliet wasn't yet ready for. And Nigel hadn't
needed a second invitation.

They were approaching the outskirts of Yonder, the
new part. Juliet couldn't help wondering where David
lived, since it was much further on. And she wondered
if it were a house, or a flat, and if he lived alone there.
Or with someone else. Someone he bought red roses for?

He suddenly stopped the car. They were still minutes
away from Deerhurst Road.

'I live just ── ' she began, about to give him
directions.

'I know where you live,' he interrupted. 'I've stopped
because I had hoped you'd give me an explanation.'

'I told you, it wasn't a very nice party.'

'Why didn't you tell the Westwood fellow you were
leaving, let him bring you home? It was his party, I
presume he invited you, it was his duty to get you home
again.' David seemed to be controlling his anger.

Juliet thought of the truth. Then she thought of her
original intention to take a taxi home.

'He'd been drinking a lot. I didn't want to risk an
accident.'

David nodded. 'Sounds reasonable. He was already

driving erratically before the party—nearly caused an accident with a Ford. Red Aston Martin, isn't it?'

She stared at him for a moment. 'You—you saw us?'

'I saw you—as the car overtook me. You wouldn't have seen me, because that idiot was driving far too fast. Oh, yes, I know all about Nigel Westwood and his reckless behaviour. The family's quite well known in these parts. Now, you can yell at me if you like, but I just don't understand what you see in the fellow. He's not your sort at all.'

Juliet swallowed. He was right, of course. But she couldn't just sit there and let him criticise her choice of friends.

'I suppose you think bringing me home gives you the right to tell me which friends I should choose, do you? Do you know Nigel personally, to say such things about him?'

'Not personally, but I know his reputation. He's a womanising playboy, that's all. I'm surprised he hasn't ditched you already, for a more sophisticated wench.'

Anger welled up in Juliet, and boiled over into words she never meant to say. 'You've got a nerve, Dr Kent! How dare you criticise my friends like that? I've met Nigel's friends, and they're all very—nice. And I shall go out with Nigel as often as I like, I shall go to his home whenever I like, and it's nothing to do with you! I don't have to ask you what I should do in my spare time, and—and I suppose now you won't want to help me find my mother, and that's all right with me, I don't care!'

Unshed tears were hurting her throat. She sat rigidly in her seat, her clothes clinging wetly to her body, and waited for him to retaliate. But his voice was calm as he said, 'I told you to yell at me, but I didn't think you would. But you have every right. You go ahead and go out with Nigel Westwood whenever you like. I just didn't realise he was your sort of person, that's all. Perhaps I've been wrong about him.'

He sounded rather sad and dejected, and Juliet found this more affecting than his previous caustic remarks.

Everything he had said was the truth, and against her will, soft tears slid down her cheeks.

'No,' she whispered, 'you were right.'

He turned towards her, holding out his arms, and she rested against his chest, feeling his warmth, smelling his manly smell. She felt she belonged there.

'What happened?' he asked gently. 'Of course, you don't have to tell me if you don't want to.'

'He — you warned me. I remember what you said. "Don't come running to me when you get hurt". I just didn't —'

She felt him stiffen. 'What did he do?'

'Do? Oh — nothing, I suppose. I just didn't feel it was right for me, not then — he was angry, disappointed in me —'

'What sort of party was it?' He spoke sharply. 'Didn't he invite anyone else?'

'Oh, yes, there were lots there, at least, at the beginning —'

'They left early, as you should have done.'

'No, they just sort of — disappeared. Upstairs, I think.' She felt the sudden tension in his body.

'Sounds like a damned orgy to me! Did you — go upstairs with him?'

'No, that's what I was trying to say! I liked Nigel — I thought I was in love with him — but then I realised, when I didn't want what he wanted, he just wasn't interested in me any more.'

David seemed to relax. 'Was he your first boyfriend?' he asked. For some reason the question put Juliet's back up.

'No, he wasn't!' She drew away from him a little. 'I'm not a child, you know, although you seem to treat me like one. I'm twenty, and I shall be a fully trained nurse in just over a year, and I'm not as innocent as you seem to imagine.

He chuckled. 'All right, all right, keep your hair on. I'm sure I never implied such a thing. But you have to admit you do look very young and innocent, so you can't blame me for putting on the Big Daddy bit.' He gently pushed a lock of hair from her face. 'I shall have to take your word for it, shan't I?' He paused, and Juliet felt he was watching her in the darkness. 'So what made you desert the sinking ship before the party was over? Why didn't you tell him you wanted to go home?'

'I — didn't know where he was.' She wasn't sure whether she should tell him the sordid details. 'I was looking for the bathroom, and I surprised him — it was an accident. He was in bed — with another girl. So I just left the house. I felt ashamed — embarrassed — ' She pulled away from him, rummaged in her pocket for a handkerchief, and couldn't find one. David produced one and handed it to her. She blew her nose noisily.

'Feel better now?'

She nodded. 'I'll wash your hanky for you.'

'Never mind that.' He seemed to be studying her intently. 'You're not seeing him again?'

'What do you think? It's just that — at first he seemed to be so nice, he was so charming, he was a lot of fun — most of the time — and I didn't realise that was all he really wanted from me. I thought — he loved me.'

He stroked her cheek gently. 'You were right — I did think you were naïve. I think perhaps you've grown up a little tonight. Grown up enough for a proper kiss, I wonder?'

Before she could reply, she was in his arms again, and his mouth was softly searching hers, his lips warm and tender, now kissing her neck, touching her face like a butterfly wing, returning to her mouth to kiss her more fervently. She felt herself responding, trying not to think of red roses, and the staff nurse on Rainbow, trying to tell herself that he was kissing her because he wanted to, because he liked her. Even if he was kissing her because he only felt sorry for her, she could pretend, couldn't she?

He slowly released her, and she lay against his arm, against the soft needlecord jacket.

'I must be making you very damp,' she murmured. David sat up quickly.

'What am I thinking about? You'll get pneumonia! Come on, I've got to get you home.'

He started the car. 'It's your fault,' he said. 'You bewitch me, you leprechaun.' He became more serious. Juliet knew his remark was just to make her feel more comfortable. 'Talking of leprechauns,' he went on, 'any news on the Elaine front since this morning?'

'Yes — I'm glad you asked. I talked to Mum, and she tried to think back to the day she met Elaine, and she remembered I was born in a nursing home in Birkleigh. Thorn House, Birkleigh.'

David glanced at her. 'Is that so? That rings a bell, somehow. I've heard of it before.'

'Yes, and I'm going there on Sunday. It's my day off. I shall check all the buses out, I'm sure —'

'I could take you. I'm off Sunday.'

'You don't really have to go to all that trouble. I shall be all right.'

'I'm sure you will. And who says it's trouble? I might like the idea of becoming an amateur detective. Your search fascinates me. Suppose you find out you're a Hungarian princess, or a Spanish countess, or — or Rasputin's secret great-granddaughter — or a descendant of the Romanovs —'

'Now you're just laughing at me!'

'Indeed I am not. I'd never do that. No, it was just my imagination running riot. Just think what a story it might make.'

'You ought to write a book.'

He turned a difficult corner skilfully. 'Perhaps I shall, one day. I think the heroine would have to be someone like you, an Irish leprechaun.'

'I told you, I'm not —'

'But you don't know, do you?'

'No, I don't know.'

'Well, here we are, and now you can change out of those awful wet things.' He stopped the car. 'I'll pick you up at ten-thirty sharp on Sunday. Be ready.'

He moved towards her, and instinctively she lifted her face for his kiss. She held her breath as their lips met, but this one was gentle and affectionate, like a brother and sister.

As the car moved away, out of sight, and she walked on air up the path to the front door, she thought, Of course, I was right before, he did just feel sorry for me, and now he's regretting kissing me the way he did. Still, it was nice while it lasted. And I am seeing him again on Sunday.

The house was dark and quiet. As she undressed for bed, almost forgetting she had probably ruined her best velvet skirt, Juliet felt warm and happy inside.

Next morning, Juliet woke to find the sun smiling cautiously between the trees. Nine-fifteen. She hadn't meant to sleep so late. Then she remembered last night, the party, the rain, David. He'd kissed her — from pity, of course, but still a kiss. She jumped out of bed, remembering the state of her black velvet skirt. It didn't look too bad; it wasn't ruined. Downstairs there were sounds of activity. Domino barked at something, and her mother called to him. Juliet stretched and smiled. She really was very lucky. She felt happy. As she dressed she found her thoughts returning again to that dreadful party. Had Nigel noticed she'd left, or hadn't he missed her at all? If he had been aware that she'd gone, he would probably have assumed that someone else had taken her home. She didn't imagine he'd have worried about it.

To think I imagined I might be falling in love with him! she thought, as she went into the kitchen. Irene was tidying up.

'I'm afraid I overslept,' Juliet apologised.

Irene smiled. 'Was it a good party? Did you get back all right? It was rather late, wasn't it? I heard you come in. Nigel must have got home very late.'

'Nigel didn't bring me home. Someone else did, who was coming this way.'

'Oh, good. It was raining, wasn't it? I heard it on the greenhouse roof.'

'Yes, it was.' Juliet fiddled with the Weetabix packet. 'Did you like Nigel, Mum?'

'Difficult to know, on first impressions. He seems very charming. Haven't had my hand kissed for a long time.' Irene chuckled. 'But I'm easily impressed by charm. Your father was more cautious, I'm afraid. Perhaps he didn't like the assumption that his casual clothes were gardening gear!' She laughed.

'It doesn't matter,' said Juliet. 'I shan't be seeing Nigel again.'

Her mother looked concerned. 'Oh, dear—what happened?'

'Nothing. I just realised I didn't like him as much as I thought, that's all. We were never serious, anyway.'

Irene hugged her. 'You're very young, Juliet. Plenty of time to find the right one. And money isn't everything.' She closed the cupboard. 'What are you having for breakfast?'

'Rather you than me,' grinned Frankie Elmore, who had a half-day. 'Hayley's mother's coming this afternoon, and I've forecast ructions.'

'I thought Hayley had accepted her mother's possible visit,' said Juliet.

'She keeps changing her mind,' put in Wendy Target. 'And I'm not sure Mrs Carter really wants to see Hayley. I think she probably feels guilty at the way her daughter was forced to leave home. I'm not sure, I'm not a psychologist.'

'How awful!' Juliet burst out. 'How can a mother not want to see her daughter?'

'You've obviously come from a happy, loving family,' said Wendy. 'When you've seen some of the problems I've seen you'll realise how lucky you are.'

'I was adopted,' said Juliet quietly. The others stared at her for a moment.

'Then you're even luckier,' said the staff nurse flatly. 'Right, Nurse Elmore, off you go.'

The junior nurse hurried away, and Wendy turned to Juliet. 'I don't think there have been any new develop-

ments since yesterday morning, but I'll run through
them to keep you up to date.' She flicked through the
Kardex. 'Mrs Cole—no further deteroriation. Dr Kent
thinks she's reached a plateau, and the odds are she
won't have to go to intensive care.'

'That's great,' enthused Juliet. So David had been on
duty this morning, had he? Juliet had been glad of her
lie-in, but it would have been nice to be here with him.
She smiled to herself, thinking of that kiss.

'Test results on Mrs Summers,' Wendy went on.
'Sarcoidosis. It's a disease of the blood and lymph
glands, more common among Afro-Caribbeans. Treatment has been started, just steroids for the moment.
She'll have to stay on them for a couple of years, more
than likely, perhaps for life. Her joints are still very
painful, but she's trying to knit something for her
husband's birthday in three weeks. She should be home
by then.'

She mentioned some other patients, then came to
Hayley Burton.

'The blood transfusion has been quite effective for the
anaemia, but she's going to need more. She's still on the
same drug regime. There's a small chance she may
recover from it with just the supportive treatment, now
the cause of the disease has been eliminated, but if she
doesn't she'll be in line for a bone marrow transplant.
She's got a brother and a younger sister, so that's a
possibility.'

'Like Donna Hazell,' said Juliet.

'Yes—they're coming this afternoon for tissue-typing.
Perhaps you'd put the stuff all ready in the treatment-
room, Nurse Avery. And then check that everyone's
ready for visitors.'

It didn't take Juliet long to lay out syringes and packs
of swabs and small dressings on a trolley. Most of the
patients, by then, were clean and fresh, perfumed and
made up, for their visitors. Juliet slipped into Donna's
room.

Donna was sitting by the window in a floral cotton

dressing-gown. She was looking very pensive, and didn't hear Juliet come in.

'Penny for them,' said Juliet. 'Or are they worth more?'

'Oh, I was just thinking — about the tissue-typing. My mother's acting very strange. She can't see the reason why she needs to have it done, since she's unlikely to be used as a donor.'

'I suppose there's always a possibility,' admitted Juliet, sitting on the bed. 'But I'm afraid I don't know too much about this sort of thing. I just know they like to do the whole family. I suppose a half-match is better than no match at all. As I said, I just don't know.'

'I just don't understand why she's so worried. It's only a needle in a vein, after all. Still, I expect David will talk her into it. He's very good at talking people into doing things.'

'I'm sure he is,' said Juliet, feeling the customary jumping of her pulse.

'Do you like him?' asked Donna suddenly.

Juliet flushed. 'He's a very good doctor, I believe,' she prevaricated.

'That's not what I asked. I asked you if you like him.'

'I do hope you're not trying to matchmake,' said Juliet. 'He's not interested in me. He likes a staff nurse on the children's ward. He takes her to the theatre.'

Donna looked surprised. 'Is that so? I didn't know.'

'And why should he tell you?'

'He tells me lots of things. Oh, I forgot to ask — how was the party last night? Your Nigel sounds like fun. What did you get up to?' Donna gave her a sidelong glance.

'I didn't get up to anything. What a mind you've got!' They both laughed.

'But he is very well off, isn't he?' Donna persisted. 'Lucky you. Still, even with all his money, I'm sure he's not as nice as penniless David. And I suppose I've upset you now, saying that.'

'Not at all. But I'm beginning to suspect you're a little in love with Dr Kent yourself.'

'Oh, yes, I always have been. But I'm just his little cousin.'

'What about Chris?'

'Oh, Chris. Yes, I'm very fond of Chris. Don't tell anyone yet! But I've grown up with David, or, should I say, I grew up idolising him. He was always around, you see. Our mothers are cousins, and there was something that happened way back when they were children—my mother saved David's mother's life, or something. They don't talk about it now. It was a long time ago.' Donna scratched her head. 'Oh, this wig itches. But I'm not keen on myself looking bald.'

Wendy put her head around the door. 'Thought I'd find you here, Nurse Avery. I want you to get a bed ready for a new patient in D. She's a diabetic, coming in for stabilisation.'

'Yes, Staff. See you later, Donna.'

The elderly diabetic lady had just been tucked into her bed when the doors were opened for visitors. They surged through the ward, laden with flowers and magazines, gradually dispersing into the various rooms. There was a constant hum of chatter, and the occasional laugh. Juliet liked visiting hours. She liked to look at the visitors as they arrived and try to match them with the patients. That pretty girl just had to be Gaynor Summer's sister, and, sure enough, that was where she went. That distinguished grey-haired man must belong to the lady with pancreatitis in H, but she was wrong there, he went into E. One out of two. That thin woman——

'Have they arrived yet?'

Juliet jumped, and flushed with surprise at David Kent's voice.

'I'm not sure I approve of the way you were looking at that visitor,' he went on, bending towards her and speaking quietly. 'He's far too old for you, for a start. And he's probably already married, unlike yours truly.'

'I wasn't——' she began, trying not to laugh out loud. 'It was just a game I was playing.'

'Then I'm not sure he'd approve,' said David, his

eyes twinkling with merriment. 'But seriously, have the Hazells arrived yet?'

'I'm not sure what they look like——'

'Not like Donna, but that's no help.' He turned as more visitors arrived, and went forward to meet them. 'Celia—Alan. How are you?'

Celia Hazell gave a nervous smile, looking to her husband to reply. Juliet was surprised to see, just as David had said, no likeness to Donna in either Celia or Alan. Perhaps she took after an aunt.

David was talking. 'We'll take the specimens in the treatment-room. I think it's all ready, isn't it, Nurse Avery?' Juliet nodded. 'Perhaps you'd come and give a hand.'

David and Alan, with the two teenaged boys, went towards the treatment-room. Celia hung back, and Juliet waited for her to draw level with her. The woman was plump, with mousy hair going grey. She wore a peach-coloured suit which only emphasised her broad hips.

'It's a bit worrying, isn't it?' she murmured as they went into the room. 'Golly, look at those needles!'

'You don't have to be scared, Mrs Hazell,' Juliet reassured her. 'It's not really painful.'

'None of us likes injections,' said Celia in a low voice. 'We think Donna's extremely brave.'

The boys were looking around with interest. The older one was tall, with reddish-fair hair, the other shorter and stocky with light brown hair like his mother. David closed the door, and gave them seats.

'You don't really need me, do you?' asked Celia tremulously, protesting to the last. David turned and smiled at her.

'And supposing you prove to be the best match for Donna? We'd never know if we didn't check.'

'Well, that would be wonderful, I know,' Celia hurried to defend her attitude. 'But it's unlikely, isn't it? I would expect Jamie or Gary to be better matches.'

'Statistically, yes,' David agreed, preparing a syringe.

'But in medicine anything can happen. And in genetics particularly.'

'That's what I mean, in a way,' murmured Celia.

'Will you fix the tourniquet, Nurse Avery?' asked David. 'We'll take Gary first — he looks bravest.'

Soon all the blood samples were taken, and labelled. David smiled at them. 'That wasn't so bad, was it? It shouldn't be long now before we know which one of you is the most suitable donor.'

'But what if——?' Celia began.

'What's wrong with you, Celia?' said Alan sharply. He was a tall, broad man with fair hair and clear hazel eyes. 'Anyone would think you don't want Donna to have a bone-marrow transplant. It may save her life!'

'I know that!' protested Celia. 'But suppose none of us matches?'

'That's certainly possible,' said David. 'But let's cross that hurdle when we come to it.' He opened the door, and they started to troop across the ward to Donna's room. Again Celia held back. At the doorway she turned to watch Juliet as she cleared the equipment away.

'Nurse Avery——' she began. Juliet was aware of the acute fear in her eyes and voice.

'I thought you'd gone,' she said. What was wrong with the woman?

'Nurse Avery, will you tell me as soon as you know, what the results are? Whether any of us is a good match or not?'

'It would be better if Dr Kent——'

'No, I don't want to wait until we come to visit. I'd rather tell Alan myself. Will you ring me and tell me, as soon as the results come back? Promise? You've got both my numbers, school and home. Will you?'

Celia looked so desperate that Juliet agreed. It wasn't ethical, but Celia seemed so terrified. 'But your husband will have to know if one of you proves to be a good match for Donna,' she added.

Celia twisted her fingers together. 'Yes, of course he will — if that should happen. But he won't need to know anything else, will he? Such as the blood-groups of us all, and the technical stuff—will he?'

'I doubt if he'd understand it,' smiled Juliet. 'I don't understand it all myself.'

'You understand about blood-groups, don't you?'

'Oh, yes, but you needn't worry about that. It's not the important factor in tissue-typing, I do know that much. Blood-groups don't have to match.'

'Oh, I didn't know that. Donna has a rare blood-group, you see. I thought it might cause problems. It does with having babies, I believe.'

'You're talking about the rhesus factor?'

'She's rhesus-negative. So's Gary and Alan.'

'That doesn't seem to be a problem,' said Juliet. 'As a matter of fact, I'm rhesus-negative myself. AB-negative, which is quite rare.'

Celia's eyes lit up. 'Like Donna! That's what they said when she first fell ill. They said it was rare.'

'You mustn't worry, Mrs Hazell. Forget about the blood-groups. It's the white cells in tissue-typing. Now, won't Donna be wondering where you are?'

'Yes. Yes, she will. But you will let me know—as soon as——'

'I will. The morning they——'

'I thought you'd got lost, Celia.' David came into the room. His gaze fixed questioningly on Juliet.

'We were just talking,' said Celia lamely. 'I'll slip along to Donna now. Is she in remission yet?'

'Nearly there. We just have to do some more throat swabs. Can't have her going down with something as soon as she's home, can we?'

Celia shook her head and left the room.

'Was something wrong?' asked David. He stood very close to Juliet, and she could smell his musky aftershave. She started to gather the syringe packets together. For a moment she'd been tempted to tell him what Celia had said. Then she remembered the woman's anxiety, and knew she had to keep it to herself. If Celia had wanted David to help she would have asked him, not an unfamiliar nurse.

'She was just worried about the transplant.'

'She should have asked me. You should have fetched me.'

'It wasn't anything technical. She didn't want you bothered. It was nothing important, really.'

He gave her a strange look. 'Staff Nurse was looking for you.' He kept his gaze on her, and she felt uncomfortable.

'Golly, I'd better run!' She hurried from the room.

Wendy was standing outside the office with a thin woman in a yellow vinyl coat. The woman was wiping her eyes on a screwed-up tissue. Juliet went up to them.

'This is Mrs Carter, Hayley's mother,' said Wendy. 'She's feeling a bit upset. Perhaps you'd take her a cup of tea in the visitors' room.'

'Sure.' Juliet went along to the kitchen where the kettle was usually boiling. She had laid the small tray when the staff nurse reappeared.

'Oh, good, you're nearly ready. You know, I was prepared to dislike the woman, but I'm beginning to feel sorry for her. She seems to have picked all the wrong men.'

Juliet glanced at her, and poured water on the tea-bags.

'Her first husband, Hayley's father, walked out on her some years ago, leaving her with three children to bring up. Hayley was heartbroken, she says. She met Mr Carter, and married him, thinking he'd be a good father for the children, but Hayley hated him from the start. Then he started to get a bit violent, but not excessive. Not until Hayley left home, then he really started — on the younger children too. So Mrs Carter took them to a refuge in Gloucester.'

Juliet was transfixed. 'How awful! I couldn't imagine a family life like that.'

'Lucky you,' said Wendy drily. 'Well, she's found them some rooms in Tewkesbury, and she wants Hayley to go back. She didn't realise Hayley was so ill, and could die.'

'Does Hayley agree to that? Going back? What about Vince?'

'That's another problem. I'm going to talk to her now. You take the tea into Mrs Carter.'

Mrs Carter was standing by the open window, smoking a cigarette. Her eyes were red. She stubbed out the cigarette and took the tea gratefully.

'I should be grateful I've found her,' she whispered. 'But I think she hates me. It wasn't her fault, it's mine—I couldn't see what he was capable of. Hayley could, she kept telling me. But he was so good to us at first—I never dreamed how he'd change——'

'Never mind. You drink your tea.' The woman drank thirstily.

Wendy came into the room. 'Finished your tea, Mrs Carter? You can come and talk to Hayley now.'

Juliet took the cup and saucer and watched them go into Room C. She waited for the shouts of anger, the loud crying, but all remained quiet. Then Wendy came out, smiling.

'Miracles?' smiled Juliet.

Wendy shrugged. 'Not quite. Both of them were wary, but at least Hayley didn't throw herself out of the window. It'll be all right. Tissue-typing all finished?'

Juliet nodded, remembering how afraid Mrs Hazell had been. And she wondered why.

CHAPTER SEVEN

'Do you think Sunday's a good day to go?' Irene placed a rack of toast on the table.

'It's as good as any,' said Juliet. 'And it's the only day I've got. Oh, yes, I know I've got tomorrow off as well, but David's off today too, and he's promised to ferry me around if I need to go from place to place.'

Juliet fished the boiled eggs from the saucepan and placed them in eggcups. Her eggcup was shaped like a chicken; she'd had it since she was a child.

'Well, I don't think you'll find many people in on a Sunday,' Irene went on. 'What do you think, Doug?' She unplugged the percolator. Douglas was reading the *Telegraph*. He looked up.

'You could be right.' He returned to the paper. Irene sat down heavily at the table.

'I've been thinking a lot about it,' she said, moving the salt cellar in a pattern on the tablecloth, 'and I think——'

'You've changed your mind! You don't want me to look for her, do you?' Juliet almost wailed.

'I promised I won't stand in your way, but I think you're rushing things. Why don't you wait and have that counselling that was suggested?'

'It's not compulsory, Mum. And what's the point? I know Elaine's name, I know where I was born—I can at least make a start. If I find I'm at a dead end, then I can ask for outside help. And, Mum, if I do find her, I shan't rush out to see her without giving her warning, I do know that much. David's going to help me. He's done this sort of thing before.'

'Who is this David?' asked Irene. 'You've mentioned him before. Is he from the hospital?'

'He's a doctor, a registrar. He comes to Melrose a lot.' Juliet peered into her fruit juice.

97

'He seems to be going to a lot of trouble to help you,' said Irene. Juliet didn't like to admit that the same thought had crossed her own mind.

'He says the idea of a search fascinates him. I think he might write a book about it one day.'

'I don't expect it will be easy,' Irene pointed out. 'It may take you weeks, months, even years. I believe it can. And supposing Elaine doesn't like the idea of a daughter from the past turning up? What will you do then?'

'I've got to risk it, Mum. Anyway, you met Elaine, you talked to her. You said yourself she didn't want to give me away, in the letter.'

'That was twenty years ago. I'm sure she didn't, at the time. But she may have accepted it by now, put it to the back of her mind.'

'And not even think of me on my birthday?' mused Juliet. 'I'm sure she wasn't like that. Mum — did she sound desperate?'

'If she was desperate,' said Irene, 'she hid it pretty well. Spun me a good story about her husband, Malcolm, and how he'd died, and she was going to stay with a friend in Birkleigh until she found a living-in job where she could keep you. Oh, she'd got it all worked out, the story she told.'

'What was the name of the friend in Birkleigh?' asked Juliet.

'She didn't say. Don't you see, if I'd known what she was really planning, I'd have asked more questions? But I didn't like to seem inquisitive.'

'I supposte not.' Juliet glanced at the clock, and pushed a last morsel of toast into her mouth. 'I'd better hurry, or I shan't be ready when David comes.' She ran upstairs, busily chewing toast.

When she returned, some twenty minutes later, she was wearing a lilac pintucked pinafore dress over a flower-sprigged blouse with a white collar. It was a warm day, so she was barelegged, with white sandals.

'Take your cable jacket,' called Irene from the

kitchen. 'Anything can happen in May. And have a nice
time.'

Juliet was studying the road map and her mother's
last words didn't register. She looked up, just as the
blue Renault drew up outside. Her heart thumped.
Excitement, she told herself; my search is beginning.
She opened the door. David was striding up the path,
his long legs encased in well-cut jeans, his broad
shoulders in a blue chambray shirt. He looked tanned
and supple, and a little smile lifted the corners of his
mouth. She found herself looking at his mouth, and
remembering. And she felt panicky. She turned to wave
to her mother.

'You look nice,' said David. He greeted her easily,
with a small kiss on her cheek. She flushed, wondering
if her mother had been watching.

'Thank you. So do you.' They walked down the path.

'Nice — and about twelve,' he added.

Juliet stared at him in dismay. She had hoped she
appeared clean and fresh, the girl-next-door image. She
knew she could never look sophisticated. But twelve!

'Oh, I'm sorry. Shall I go and change?'

'Whatever for? You look — exquisite. But very, very
young. I know — you're my niece. I can pretend to be
your uncle David. How about that?'

'I think your imagination has gone too far. I absolutely refuse to call you Uncle!'

They laughed, and he opened the car door for her.
Juliet couldn't help thinking how elegant Moira Charles
always appeared to be, never a blonde hair out of place,
never a crease in her dress. No wonder David liked her.
He would never pretend she was his niece!

Her hand stroked the soft upholstery of the car. It
was only two days since she had sat in this same seat
and dribbled raindrops everywhere. Strange that David
should be coming along at that very moment that she'd
emerged on to the main road. Waiting? She had wondered about it.

She watched his hands as he started the car, firm but

sensitive on the wheel. Hands that had held her as he
kissed her —— Stop it! she told herself.

'Did you tell your parents I was taking you out
today?' David asked casually.

'I mentioned it.' She tried to match his nonchalance.

'They didn't mind a stranger getting involved in your
family concerns?'

'But you're not a stranger!' Juliet said quickly.
'You're——'

'A friend?' He spoke softly, his eyes on the road.

'Of course—a friend. A colleague.'

'Oh, I see.'

'I told them you could be quite helpful because you
knew someone who had traced her natural mother.'

'Yes, I do.'

'How marvellous for her. Such a satisfying, happy
ending!'

David didn't answer. He braked as a Metro cut in
front of him, and swore under his breath. He switched
on the radio and they listened without speaking for a
while, and Juliet forgot he hadn't answered her last
statement. A news programme started.

'Do you know the way to Birkleigh?' Juliet asked,
fishing out her map.

'Yes, I've been a number of times.' He lowered the
radio. 'Your mention of Thorn House rang a little bell
with me. I'm positive my grandmother worked there
until she retired. She was a midwife, you see.'

Juliet felt an excited tremor run through her.

'Do you think she might have met Elaine?' She was
afraid to breathe.

'I suppose it's a possibility. But she must have
delivered hundreds of babies. I'm sure she can't have
remembered them all.'

'You don't think we could ask her? She is still alive?'

David laughed. 'Very much alive, and kicking! I visit
her now and again. She still drives her car. She's not
ancient, you know. Did you think perhaps I was too old
to have a grandmother still alive?'

'Oh, no, I wasn't thinking that at all!'

'I'm twenty-nine in June, a couple of weeks' time—not quite elderly. Although to someone of your tender years I suppose I do seem quite old and decrepit.' His mouth twitched.

'Twenty-nine is a nice age,' said Juliet politely, ignoring the wry humour in his voice. 'But I'm not really so young. I'm out of my teens.'

'Twenty, I think you said. But only just, I imagine.'

'April—April the tenth.'

He nodded, turning the car in the direction of Pershore. Within minutes they were travelling under the motorway. The sun was shining, the air was warm, and the low murmurs from the radio were beginning to make Juliet feel drowsy. The newsreader mentioned a child who had gone to the States for a life-saving operation, a vital double transplant that had never been done in Britain. And Juliet suddenly remembered Donna, and Mrs Hazell's frightened face came to her mind.

'David?' she said suddenly.

'Oh, you are awake, then.'

'I was only thinking.'

'Do you always snore while you think?'

'I wasn't snoring! I don't snore—I wasn't asleep. I don't think I snore.'

He laughed. 'I'm just teasing. What were you thinking?'

'About Donna, and her bone marrow transplant.'

'Mmm. She's pretty well banking on Jamie or Gary being a perfect match. I only hope to God one of them is.'

He spoke fervently. Juliet thought of Donna being a bit in love with him, and she wondered how he felt about her.

'When will the tissue-typing results be ready?'

'Oh, it doesn't take long—a few days. Could even be tomorrow, I suppose, but it's more likely to be Tuesday or Wednesday.'

'I've got another day off tomorrow,' said Juliet.

'Lucky you. I haven't.'

'Oh, I didn't mean—I'm really very grateful to you,

giving up your day off for me. I didn't expect you to do
the same again — that is, if you had a day off tomorrow.'

She sat there feeling awkward. But what had suddenly
occurred to her was that, with her having a day off
tomorrow, if the tissue-typing results came she wouldn't
be able to ring Mrs Hazell, as she'd promised. And now
David would be thinking she wanted him to take her
out again. She did, of course, but she couldn't tell him
that.

'You don't have to feel grateful,' he said. 'I thought
I'd explained that I'm doing it because I want to.'

Of course! The detective work fascinated him. It was
nothing to do with herself. As long as she remembered
that.

They were approaching Birkleigh. Population four
thousand; a pleasant, unspoiled village, there still
existed thatched cottages, Cotswold stone houses
Naples-yellow in the sunlight, and black and white half-
timbered dwellings with long histories. They drove
slowly along the main street, Juliet too tense to see the
pretty shops selling antiques and gifts. So far none of
the houses they had seen qualified as commercial prop-
erties, and Juliet began to have a sinking feeling,
remembering what her mother had said. Suppose Thorn
House had been pulled down?

'Last time I came,' David was saying, as they turned
left at the end of the main road, 'I think I remember
some larger houses along here.' Not far ahead, they
could see the banks of the Avon, and families having
picnics. In the distance, anglers sat motionless with
fishing rods.

David had been right, thought Juliet excitedly, as
they approached the first of a row of huge old houses.
The road was narrow, so he stopped the car and they
got out. Juliet almost ran to the first house, which
sported a wooden sign behind a straggly hawthorn
hedge. Chestnut House, Residential Home for the
Elderly, it read. Remnants of another name showed
faintly through. Juliet stared at it. Was that a T? And

an H? David came and stood behind her. She turned and looked at him, a question in her eyes.

'I don't think so,' he said slowly. 'And it's very dilapidated.'

It was. Although the leaded windows remained intact, the paint was flaking and chipped, and the place had a neglected air.

'Let's look at the others,' suggested David. He took her hand, and a warm feeling spread through her. She was appreciative of his presence.

The next house had been modernised, and painted in vivid blue and white. It proudly boasted that it was the Jack-in-the-Box Private Kindergarten, for children aged 2–5 years. Brightly coloured shapes adorned the windows, and, as they passed, Juliet caught sight of a climbing frame and an inflated rubber castle at the rear of the house.

David urged her on, ignoring her quizzical glance. The next house was now offices for a computer firm. It was clean and efficient-looking in black and white.

'Look,' said David.

Juliet saw the sign before she saw the house. It was partly hidden by cypress trees and a high hedge, but the sign had been newly painted in dark green, and there was no doubting it: Thorn House. She had found it. Excitement tightened her throat. She turned to David.

'Come on,' he said. 'What are you waiting for?'

The house was double-fronted, painted cream, with a wide dusty drive approaching from the left-hand side. In front of the house was a large square lawn that needed cutting, and at the far side a row of straggly flowers, mostly lupins, with some poppies and columbines.

The front door was open, revealing a stone-flagged porch, and an inner door with frosted glass in the top half. As they stepped into the porch, Juliet heard a voice from inside, calling stridently to someone named Margaret. She turned and smiled at David, and he gave her arm an encouraging squeeze.

'Margaret, what do you think you're doing?' the voice

went on. 'I thought I told you to do the potatoes? What are you doing with that colander?'

'I don't hear any babies crying,' Juliet said quietly, and pressed the bell.

'Probably just been fed,' said David. 'And that reminds me, where shall we go for lunch?'

Lunch was the last thing on Juliet's mind at that moment: she was far too excited. The inner door opened, and a square-shaped woman in a brown overall stood glaring at them.

'Are you the social worker?' she demanded of David. 'Because I've already told Mr Priest we just don't have room for any more, unless you want them to sleep in the cellar. We wanted to send Doreen to her family, but they don't want her after all——'

'We're not social workers, Miss——Mrs——' began Juliet quickly.

'Wimbush——Edna Wimbush. Who are you, then? You realise this is Sunday?'

While listening to Mrs Wimbush's diatribe, Juliet had slowly come to realise that although this was Thorn House it was no longer the maternity home Elaine had known. Standing behind Mrs Wimbush, colander in hand, was a heavy-browed, dark-haired woman in a drab, shapeless frock, and on her face the perplexed expression of the mentally confused.

'I'm sorry to have bothered you, Mrs Wimbush,' said Juliet, stepping back. 'We seem to have come to the wrong place.' She turned quickly, anxious that David shouldn't see the sudden tears in her eyes.

'Wait a minute, Juliet.' He grasped her arm firmly.

'I wish you'd tell me what you want,' said Mrs Wimbush sharply. 'I can't stay on this doorstep all day——I've got the lunches to supervise. And they need supervision, I can tell you!' Behind her, Margaret laughed.

'That's what I mean!' Juliet burst out, her eyes bright. 'This isn't a maternity home any more!'

'Maternity home?' Mrs Wimbush stared at them.

'You're looking for a maternity home?' She glanced at Juliet's slim figure.

'I believe this was a maternity home once?' asked David, his hand still on Juliet's arm.

'Well, yes, it was, but that was a few years ago. Then it became a residential nursery before the social services took it over five years ago.'

'Social services?' echoed Juliet.

'We take ex-psychiatric patients who aren't yet ready to go into the community. It's a hostel now, and I'm the housekeeper.'

'It's a dead end, David. Our first lead, and it's a dead end. Come on, let's go home.' Tears were dangerously near the surface, and Juliet bit her lip to keep control.

'Wait,' said David. 'Don't give up so soon.' She could hear the concern in his voice, and her lower lip quivered.

'Are you in charge?' he asked Mrs Wimbush.

'Only the domestic side, teaching them cooking and cleaning and laundry and such. It's not an easy task. Mrs Taylor's the superintendent, but it's Sunday, and she's off. Miss Pope's here, to keep an eye on things.'

'How long has she worked here?' asked David.

'Oh, right from the beginning. Lives in the village, always has done, and her family — she knows everybody, does Miss Pope.'

'She may be just the person we need,' said David, glancing meaningfully at Juliet. Juliet's spirits began to rise. 'May we see her?'

'I'll go and see if I can find her,' said Mrs Wimbush. 'She was giving Jessie her insulin injection not long ago. She may be back in the office. Wait here.'

They stood in the square, tiled hall with its functional teak furniture. Margaret stood looking at them belligerently. David crossed to examine a Victorian print, smiling at Margaret as he did so. The woman muttered something and stared at Juliet.

'Hello, Margaret,' said Juliet, a little disconcerted when the woman lifted the colander and held it before her.

'What's your name?' Margaret demanded. Juliet had

an awful suspicion that she was about to strike her with the plastic colander, and she stepped back.

'Juliet. My name's Juliet.'

The woman laughed harshly. David glanced across and smiled, and Juliet shot him an agonised glance which he didn't intercept.

'Romeo—where are you, Romeo?' Margaret laughed again and went right up to Juliet, who held her breath. The woman inspected her, her head on one side, then she reached out with her free hand, and gently stroked Juliet's shining black hair.

'Nice,' she said. 'Nice.' Juliet breathed a sigh of relief. Just then Mrs Wimbush reappeared.

'Come away, Margaret, and do those potatoes,' she said sharply. Then, to Juliet and David, 'Miss Pope will see you, but she's very busy, and she would have preferred to know what it's all about.'

'We shan't take much of her time,' David promised.

'It's down that corridor—there, second door on the left. Come along, Margaret, what's wrong with you today?'

Juliet and David crossed the hall. 'What's the point?' whispered Juliet.

'The point is, she's from the village. She'll remember Thorn House when it was a nursing home, and probably the people who worked here then.'

'Do you think it's worth a try?'

'Don't you? Come on.' He took her hand and they approached the second door on the left. Juliet tapped in, and a voice told them to go in.

Miss Pope was quite elderly, rather like a white-haired bird. Her small round eyes darted glances at them.

'Mrs Wimbush tells me you expected to find Thorn House still a maternity home. Sit down—that's right, there.'

They sat on vinyl-upholstered chairs facing her across the desk. Miss Pope gave them a quick smile.

'I'm looking for someone who had a baby here, twenty years ago,' said Juliet.

'Rather a long shot, wasn't it? Twenty years? How do you know the baby was born here?'

'It's the only lead I have——' Juliet swallowed, looked at David for support. He smiled. 'The fact is, I was that baby, and I know I was born here twenty years ago——'

'I guessed that.' Miss Pope nodded.

'I was adopted, and I'm trying to trace my mother. I know her name, and I thought this was a good place to start.'

'The best place—at the beginning. Did you think I might have been here then?'

Juliet nodded, and David squeezed her hand. Miss Pope saw it and smiled.

'This is your boyfriend, I suppose? You want to find your roots before you get married, is that it?'

Juliet felt her cheeks redden. She was too embarrassed to look at David, but she knew he must be amused.

'Something like that,' she heard him say quietly, and it was all she could do to stop herself looking amazed.

'Of course I remember Thorn House when it was a maternity home. I've always lived in Birkleigh. I wasn't actually born in Thorn House, it wasn't a maternity home that long ago——' she gave a wry smile '—but I do remember when it opened, some time in the Forties, just after the war, when mothers started having their babies away from home. I was nursing at Tewkesbury General then——' Her eyes grew misty, and Juliet and David exchanged glances.

'I had to leave when my father died, to look after my mother, and it wasn't until the late Sixties that I was free to go back to work. I went to Pershore Cottage Hospital. It's by the cricket ground—do you know it?'

They shook their heads. The palms of Juliet's hands felt damp. Was this rigmarole going to lead anywhere, or would it really be a dead end?

'And then Thorn House became a nursery,' Miss Pope went on. 'Well, mothers were having their babies in hospital, I can't think why—they wanted all the technology and epidurals and things. Not enough facilities here, you see.'

'And then the social services took it over,' prompted David.

'That's right.' She looked brightly at them. Was that it? thought Juliet.

'You never worked here yourself—until now——?' she asked desperately.

'Five years ago, when it re-opened. It was nearer for me. It's a bit stark now, compared with what it was like when Miss Rose was here. She made it lovely.'

'Miss Rose?' They spoke simultaneously.

'The matron when it was a maternity home. I never actually met her, but I've seen her around, and I heard a lot about her. She was very well liked.'

'What happened to her?' asked Juliet, and held her breath.

'She retired, the day it closed. She was in her sixties. She lives here in the village, at the other end. As I said, I only know her by sight, and, now you mention it, I haven't seen her around lately.'

Juliet's heart sank. 'Do you think she'd have met my mother?'

'Twenty years ago? Well, she was here then. She lives at the other end, Blackberry Lane, I'm not sure of the number, but I was told she has a monkey puzzle tree in her front garden. Strange things, monkey puzzle trees.'

'Yes,' they agreed. Juliet stood up. Not a wasted journey, after all, but she was anxious to carry on. David glanced at his watch.

'I hope we haven't taken too much of your time,' he apologised.

'Not at all. Glad to help.' They turned to go. 'I hope you find your mother.'

'Thank you.' They looked at each other when they reached the corridor outside. Juliet was too excited to speak, but her eyes told it all.

'It's quarter to twelve,' said David. 'Do you want to see Miss Rose before we have lunch or after?'

'Blow lunch!' Juliet burst out, 'I want to find out more!'

He grinned understandingly, and they hurried from the house. Juliet stopped on the drive and looked back.

'The house where I was born,' she said wistfully. 'I wonder what Elaine thought when she saw it?'

'Probably. Let's get this over as soon as possible!' said David. Juliet laughed, and they walked back to the car.

'I do hope she remembers,' Juliet murmured fervently as they sat down.

'Don't pin your hopes on it,' warned David. His brown eyes were full of understanding, and something else she didn't recognise. He rested his hand on hers. It felt warm and reassuring. 'I don't want to see you hurt,' he said softly.

'You keep saying that, but why should I get hurt? Disappointed, perhaps, if I don't find her — but I intend to, David, I intend to find her! How can that hurt me?'

He gazed at her without speaking, then started the car. 'Just don't expect too much,' he said quietly, as the car began to move away. Juliet could still feel the pressure of his hand. She said nothing.

They drove through the village, and she admired a picturesque thatched cottage. 'Just like a chocolate box, or a jigsaw puzzle,' she remarked. They found Blackberry Lane right at the end, on the right-hand side. The cottages were old, with small windows and in front of the last cottage sat a monkey puzzle tree.

'This is it,' breathed Juliet, as she left the car and opened the small white gate. David followed her up the short path between the borders of spring flowers. Juliet knocked at the door. It reverberated in the small house. A young woman opened the door. She held a plump baby of about seven months on her hip, and a toddler clutched at her cotton skirt. She was rosy-cheeked and very young. Not Miss Rose.

'I'm sorry, I thought Miss Rose lived here,' Juliet began.

'The old lady who was a matron? Oh, no, dear, she doesn't live here any more.'

'She's not —— ?' Juliet couldn't say the word.

'Dead? Oh, no, not as far as I know. She went to live in Pershore — a bungalow in Pershore. For her legs, you see. Better for her legs.'

Juliet turned to David. 'She's not here.'

'A bungalow in Pershore,' the young woman reiterated. 'She's been gone nearly two years. Sorry I can't help you more. Pershore — it's not far.'

'No,' David agreed, 'it's not far.'

CHAPTER EIGHT

THEY sat in the car for a few minutes without speaking. 'Do you think it might be third time lucky?' Juliet said finally in a hesitant voice.

'Are you discouraged already?' asked David.

'It seems like one dead end after another, that's all.'

'My dear girl, you've hardly started! Did you really expect to find your mother on the first day? It could take months!'

'I know!' wailed Juliet. 'I'm trying not to think of it. I thought we'd got such a good start, knowing my mother's name and where I was born.'

'You know more than most. Think yourself lucky. Right, off we go to Pershore.' He started the car.

Juliet sat rigidly in her seat. She knew she was being unreasonable, and she was worried she might alienate David. And how would she get to all these places so quickly without him?

'I'm sorry,' she said. He glanced at her. They were leaving the village, crossing the Avon.

'Sorry? For what?'

'For expecting too much. For taking you for granted.'

'What makes you think you're taking me for granted?' His hands were lean and sure on the wheel. His dark curly hair was becoming tousled.

'Well, to be honest, by now I expected you to be shrugging your shoulders and turning the car for home. I couldn't have complained if you had.'

'My dear Juliet, how many more times do I have to tell you I'm doing this because it interests me? And besides, I like being in the company of a pretty girl, even if she does look only twelve.' He gave her a sidelong glance.

'Do I really look so young?'

'Obviously not. Miss Pope assumed you were my

girlfriend. Of course, she may have secretly thought I
was cradle-snatching, but she was too well-bred to say
anything.' He quivered with uncontrolled mirth, and
Juliet found herself smiling. It was impossible to stay
grumpy with David Kent around.

'I told you I was interested as soon as you mentioned
Birkleigh and Thorn House, didn't I?' he went on. 'I
felt I wanted to be part of it. Don't ask me why, I don't
know myself, it was just a hunch I had. So let's have no
more of this taking-me-for-granted stuff, all right? I'm
here because I want to be, because I like your company,
and I think we should be enjoying it. So shall we?'

'Yes, let's,' Juliet agreed reluctantly. He grinned at
her.

It didn't take long to reach Pershore. As they drove
along Three Springs Road, Juliet suddenly realised they
didn't know Miss Rose's address! She turned to David.

'How do you know where to go, David? We don't
know her address.'

'We're aiming for a telephone box — a phone book, to
be exact. And if she isn't in, we'll cruise round looking
for bungalows. Pershore isn't a big place. Ah — a
garage.' He stopped on the forecourt and jumped out.
'Shan't be long.'

He disappeared inside, and Juliet saw his dark head
bent over something. He spoke to the cashier, and was
soon back with something in his hand. He dropped it
on Juliet's lap and started the car. A street map. Juliet
unfolded it.

'Number nine, Gracecourt,' he said as they turned
back to the street. 'Near the cricket ground. This way, I
think.'

Juliet scanned the map. It was very clear to read.
'Down here — past the Abbey on the right — a bit further — slowly now —'

Gracecourt was next to the cricket ground. At the
other side was the Cottage Hospital Miss Pope had
mentioned. The bungalows were small and neat, laid in
a semi-circle with small squares of garden at the front,

facing a central green with benches and even a small pond.

'How pretty,' murmured Juliet as they left the car. 'Let's hope she's at home.'

The door of number nine was green and spotless. Juliet knocked, and a lace curtain twitched. Her heart began to race as she rehearsed what she was going to say. Next to her, David had his fingers crossed, and she smiled to herself. How could she ever have doubted his motives?

The door opened a short way, and a small elderly lady with soft cotton-wool hair peered out at them. She had bright blue eyes that surveyed them warily. She gazed at Juliet, and a puzzled frown crossed her brow.

'Yes?' she said at last.

'I hope we're not disturbing you at lunchtime,' Juliet began.

'I've had my lunch—I eat early. What is it you want?'

Juliet plunged right in, forgetting what she had rehearsed. 'I'm looking for someone who gave birth to a baby at Thorn House.'

Miss Rose frowned. 'Thorn House? The place closed fifteen years ago.'

'Yes, I know.' Juliet cast David a desperate glance.

'Miss Rose, we must introduce ourselves,' he said. 'I'm David Kent, I'm a registrar at Riverside General Hospital, and this is Juliet Avery, she's a nurse.'

'Well, I suppose I shall have to believe you.' Miss Rose opened the door wider. 'There are all sorts of people trying to rob and cheat you, but you sound like a doctor, and you, young lady, could never get away with a crime. You'd better come in.'

Not sure whether she should treat the remark as a compliment or not, Juliet followed her into the house with David, and Miss Rose closed the front door. 'You'd better sit down and tell me what you want me to do.'

The cosy living-room was small and cluttered. Every surface was covered with photographs, many of them old, but all of them of women with babies. It was quite

obvious where Miss Rose's interests still lay. There were
brass ornaments on the mantelpiece, and an antique
French clock in ormolu.

The old lady came in and sat down. 'Fire away,' she
said briskly, and Juliet glimpsed the efficient matron
she must have been.

'I was born at Thorn House twenty years ago,' she
began. 'I was adopted, and I'm looking for my real
mother.'

'My dear, your real mother has been looking after
you for the past twenty years,' said Miss Rose sharply.
'You mean your natural mother.'

Juliet flushed. 'Yes, of course. I meant to say that.'

'You're looking for your roots — I quite understand.
But do you really expect me to remember babies who
were born twenty years ago?'

Juliet gestured towards the photographs. 'You appear
to have kept in touch with many of them.'

'I only know who they are because their names are
on the back,' admitted Miss Rose. 'I delivered
hundreds, and I met hundreds more while I was matron
of Thorn House. You can tell me your mother's name,
and I will do my best.'

'Elaine Webb,' said Juliet. 'I think she was a widow.'

Miss Rose stared at her, then shook her head. 'For a
moment then I thought you were going to give me a
different name. I'm sorry, dear, I don't know that name
at all. What day were you born?'

'April the tenth.'

'Twenty years ago, April. Ah, that was the time we
had a spring flu epidemic. Now I do remember that.
Half my staff were off sick. The tenth — what day of the
week —— ?'

'Friday,' said Juliet, desperation creeping into her
voice.

'Weekend,' mused Miss Rose. 'I do remember one
weekend, during the flu outbreak, must have been early
April — yes, a girl in prolonged labour, we were all
getting worried about her, she nearly lost her baby. I
was off duty and Kate was alone, on night duty ——'

She seemed to be rambling, and Juliet wanted to prompt her, get her back to the subject.

Miss Rose meandered on. 'Yes, the other nurse was off sick, the doctor couldn't get there on time, he was out on a call, poor little thing——'

Juliet had noticed how David had looked up sharply while Miss Rose was talking. Now he interrupted.

'Did you say Kate?' he asked. Miss Rose swivelled her head to look at him.

'That's right. The midwife, Kate Maybury. One of my most reliable nurses. Never let me down—wonderful woman! She delivered the baby, resuscitated it—and remember, we didn't have all the fancy equipment the hospitals did. The baby came out of it right as rain. It was a little girl, I believe. And now I come to think——' Miss Rose got up with some difficulty and crossed to an oak bureau. She opened a drawer. 'Got them here somewhere.' She sat down again, and pulled the rubber band from a bundle of photographs. 'I didn't get round to putting them all in frames. But I'm sure she sent me a picture. Of the seaside, I think.'

She shuffled through the pile, scattering them around her. 'Can't think why I'm showing you this, it's nothing to do with your mother. Ah, here we are!' She passed the snapshot to Juliet, who took it with feigned interest.

The subject of the photograph was a plain, round-faced woman in a spotted frock, sitting on a wall, with the sea behind her. She seemed vaguely familiar to Juliet, and she stared at her for a moment, trying to place where she might have seen her. On her knee, she held a small, dark-haired baby. The baby was frowning. The mother was eating an ice-cream cone.

Casually, Juliet turned it over and read the words. And her heart seemed to stop.

Celia Hazell and baby Donna, born April 10th. Isn't she a bonny baby now, Miss Rose?

David was watching her. 'Is something wrong, Juliet?' he asked quickly. Wordlessly, she passed the photo-

graph to him. He read the message on the back and his
face changed.

'Kate Maybury delivered this baby, Miss Rose?' he
asked quietly.

'That's right. The baby who nearly didn't make it.'

'Kate Maybury is my grandmother, Miss Rose. And
Celia Hazell is her niece, a sort of cousin of mine.'

Miss Rose took the photograph and scrutinised it. 'So
she delivered her niece's baby. I wasn't aware of that,
but then there was no one else. The doctor came too
late to do it. And she made a jolly good job of it.'

'She did.'

Juliet was remembering Celia's frightened voice as
she asked her to tell her the blood results before anyone
else. That dark-haired baby, Donna, looked nothing like
Alan — or Celia —— What was she thinking? That Celia
had cheated on her husband? It would explain her
panic, her anxiety.

She saw again the words on the back of the snapshot:
Baby Donna, born April 10th. Donna Hazell had been
born at Thorn House on the same day as herself! She
was surprised she hadn't noticed the coincidence when
she'd looked at Donna's file. Perhaps it just hadn't
registered.

'Miss Rose,' she began, unsure how to phrase it,
'You've just said you remember the birth of Celia
Hazell's ——'

'Oh, no, I wasn't there when she delivered,' the ex-
matron reminded her. 'I was expecting a relief nurse to
arrive, and the doctor who'd been sent for. I had no
doubt they'd turn up within a short time, so I went off
duty. I think there was an orderly or somebody. And
Mrs Hazell was going so slowly, she wasn't expected to
deliver within the next hour or so, and anyway, I had
an important appointment to keep.'

'I don't think we're criticising you for that,' put in
David.

'Oh, no,' said Juliet. 'But if you remember Celia
Hazell, surely you remember the other mothers who
delivered around that time?'

'Mothers in the plural?' said Miss Rose, her eyebrows raised. 'We rarely had more than a couple of deliveries a day—we didn't have the space. I'm almost sure we had no deliveries before Mrs Hazell that day. The reason I remember her is because she took so long. What was that name you told me? Eileen?'

'Elaine Webb,' said Juliet.

'Elaine. It doesn't mean anything to me at all.'

Juliet slumped in her chair. So near and yet so far. It was her own fault for expecting too much. David noticed her dejected attitude, and got up.

'I'm sorry we've taken so much of your time, Miss Rose,' he said politely. 'It was kind of you to try to help, and a pity you can't help us further. I'm sure you've done your best.'

Miss Rose got up, and snapshots fell to the carpet. 'I shall try to remember,' she promised them. 'Leave me your telephone number, and if I do remember something I'll ring you. Sorry I can't promise more than that.'

'That's very kind of you,' said Juliet, holding out her hand. David was busy writing down the phone number on a piece of paper. It crossed Juliet's mind that she'd never given him her home number, so how could he know it?

At the front door, Miss Rose said, 'Have you thought of talking to Kate Maybury? I'm sure she'd talk to you, Dr Kent. And she's probably the only other one who could have delivered your young lady here.'

Juliet's eyes shone. Miss Rose's suggestion that she was David's 'young lady' passed unnoticed. But David's grandmother! Hadn't she suggested it herself earlier? Now it seemed even more likely that she was the one who would know.

'She's right, David. Your grandmother should know.'

'You know where she lives?' asked Miss Rose. 'But of course you do. Tewkesbury.'

'That's right.' They said goodbye and returned to the car.

'Tewkesbury's on our way back,' said Juliet.

'It may be but I intend to eat first. Let's see if we can find a pub.'

Luckily they weren't very far from an inn which overlooked the river, and, although Juliet enjoyed her scampi and salad, she couldn't help feeling restless, and impatient to get away.

David relaxed over his Dover sole, and sipped leisurely at his mineral water. He glanced with amusement at Juliet's fidgeting.

'You're like a cat on hot bricks,' he remarked.

She tried to relax. 'I know. I can't help it. I've learned one thing, and I want to know more.'

'What do you think you've learned?'

'That your grandmother delivered me, so she must have known Elaine.'

David frowned. 'There you go again, jumping to conclusions. Miss Rose admitted she didn't remember much of that day, except for Celia's long labour — which I did know about, but it slipped my mind — so it's possible she's forgotten other deliveries during the day, when there were other midwives on duty. My grandmother may not have delivered you at all.'

Juliet pulled a face. 'All right. But she'd have been there! She'd have met my mother!'

'As Miss Rose did. But didn't remember.'

'Oh, David, why are you trying to spoil it for me? I thought you were on my side!'

He gently held her hand on the table. 'It's not a question of sides, Juliet. But you may be spoiling it for yourself. Don't expect anything, and you may be pleasantly surprised — that's my philosophy. Especially in a situation like this. I don't want to see it end in tragedy.'

He was leaning across the table, and his face was very close to hers. His brown eyes seemed to be saying things again, things she wanted to hear him speak. Could he be afraid to put them into words? She was tense, almost afraid to breathe, almost afraid to meet his gaze. Then he sat back and the spell was broken.

'Must come here again,' he said brightly. 'Are you ready?'

They were both aware of the tense vibrations between them, and during the journey back to Tewkesbury both seemed determined to keep the conversation light and easy. Various patients cropped up, inevitably, and Hayley Burton was one of them.

'The strange thing is,' David admitted, 'I quite like that Vince fellow. He's very fond of Hayley, but they're both lost creatures and need a lot of guidance.'

'Do you think they'll give up glue-sniffing?' asked Juliet, more comfortable with this subject.

'They have to. It's almost killed Hayley. We hope she won't need a bone-marrow transplant. Actually, about half of known aplastic anaemias recover without one. She may be one of the lucky ones. And I'd like to think Vince will have more sense than to put temptation in her way.'

Chatting like this, the journey passed quickly, and soon they had reached Tewkesbury.

'I have to admit,' said David, as they drove along Ashchurch Road, 'I've neglected my grandmother lately. It sounds a lame excuse, I know, but I never seem to be able to find the time. Things seem to crop up when I'm off duty.'

'Like chasing round the country looking for my mother,' said Juliet, with a wry smile, and he laughed.

'Yes, you're quite right. Well, now we can kill two birds with one stone. Bit of a cliché, I know. And here we are.' He stopped the car outside a small cottage in Manor Crescent, which led off Queens Road.

'Dinky houses,' said David, as they approached the front door. 'But some of the rear gardens—and my grandmother's is one of them—lead right down to the river.'

'The Avon?'

'The Swilgate. It joins up with the Mill Avon.' He rang the bell. A dog barked, then stopped.

'Visiting day,' murmured Juliet.

'Sorry?'

'It's our visiting day, not the patients'. I've never

visited so many people in one——' The door opened,
and Kate Maybury gave a delighted exclamation.

'David!' She leaned forward and kissed him. 'Do
come in! I've just made a cuppa. Come and join me.'

Her glance alighted on Juliet, and a confused
expression crossed her plump features.

'This is Juliet, Granny. She's a nurse at the hospital.'

'How nice.' They shook hands and went inside.

The sitting-room was very small, as David had said,
and had a country look about it, with lots of chintz and
dried flowers, and old cherrywood furniture. A small
dog basket stood near the hearth. Juliet and David sat
in squashy armchairs while Mrs Maybury fetched the
tray of tea. She had added a plate of home-made cake.

Juliet wasn't really hungry, but she politely accepted
a small slice.

'I was only thinking about you the other day, David,'
said his grandmother, settling herself in a high-backed
chair, her feet planted firmly on the floral Axminster
carpet. She was a heavily-built woman with grey hair
cut quite short, and she wore rimless spectacles. The
sort who stood no nonsense, thought Juliet, and she
could imagine her as a ward sister.

'I know I should have come before now, but I've been
very busy,' said David, with a sidelong glance at Juliet.
Her heart gave a little jump at his intimate smile.

'I thought you might call and tell me about Donna,'
Mrs Maybury went on. 'I'm very worried about her.
Celia promised to let me know, but I haven't seen her
for weeks.'

'You should have rung her, Granny. She's busy too, I
expect, visiting the hospital and teaching full-time.'

'You know how I feel about Celia, David. I didn't
want to worry her unnecessarily. She has enough to
think about.'

'Well, Donna's coming along fine,' David told her.
'Isn't that right, Juliet?' He smiled encouragingly, and
Juliet was gratified by his attempt to include her in the
conversation. She nodded.

'Almost in remission,' she agreed.

'She had a strong cocktail of chemotherapy,' added David. 'And she'll soon be home. Just a few throat bugs to deal with.'

'I'm a bit out of touch with this modern medicine,' Kate Maybury admitted. 'Does that mean she's cured? Celia said something about a bone-marrow transplant, but that was weeks ago. Does she still need it?'

'It's on the cards,' David agreed. 'But Jamie or Gary should prove to be suitable donors. They were tested yesterday.'

Kate licked her lips. 'Are siblings always good matches?'

'Not always. Usually, but it's not a certainty.'

'Oh, I see.' She smiled. 'And how are you getting on? Has Martin got a new girlfriend?'

The conversation drifted into family chat, and Kate Maybury seemed to relax.

'My, this cake is good!' David commented, and Juliet murmured her agreement. 'We get nothing like this at the hospital.'

'You'll have to visit me more often,' said his grand-mother, a twinkle in her eye. It was obvious to Juliet that she thought the world of David.

'There's something we want to ask you, Granny,' said David. 'Well, Juliet does.'

For a brief moment the old lady's gaze rested on her, and Juliet thought she glimpsed a flicker of fear. Then Mrs Maybury smiled and turned back to her grandson.

'You see, Granny,' David went on, as it seemed she was expecting him to explain, 'Juliet was born at Thorn House, twenty years ago, on the same day as Donna, and she's — oh —!'

Kate had somehow knocked over her cup, and tea spilled on to the tray, splashing her skirt.

'It's all right, David, I'm just being clumsy, as usual. It comes with old age.' She dabbed at her skirt with a handkerchief. 'Go on — I'm listening.' She avoided look-ing at Juliet, even though the latter was the subject of the discussion.

'Juliet was adopted, and she's trying to trace her

mother. She has the idea that you probably delivered her.'

'Oh, no, I'm sure I didn't!' Mrs Maybury's reaction was instantaneous. David looked puzzled.

'How can you be so sure, Granny? You delivered Donna, didn't you?'

There was a short pregnant silence, and Juliet could feel the uneasiness in the room. Something was wrong.

'Did Celia tell you, David?' asked his grandmother quietly.

'No, Miss Rose did. We've just come from her house.'

'Miss Rose. I see.' She fixed her gaze finally on Juliet, a hostile gaze. She spoke in a brusque voice. 'Have you stopped to think this thing out, Juliet? Have you considered the harm you may be causing to people, tearing up the past in this way? Is it so vital to you that you find your mother? I'm sure you have perfectly good adoptive parents who think the world of you. Are you willing to risk all they've given you?'

Juliet was completely taken aback, and even David looked puzzled and shocked. And then it crossed her mind that Kate Maybury must be afraid, anxious that Juliet shouldn't find out what she wanted. But why? She found her voice.

'My parents are quite agreeable to my looking for my roots, Mrs Maybury. And yes, it is very important to me. Miss Rose told us you were on duty that night, when Donna was born. And I was born the same day. Even if you didn't deliver me yourself, you must have met my mother.'

The old lady sighed. 'Perhaps I did. But I must have met thousands of mothers in my career. Why should I remember yours? What was her name?'

'Elaine Webb.' Juliet watched her, waiting for her reaction. Mrs Maybury seemed to subside in her chair, and an expression of relief crossed her face. She shook her head, her mouth quivering in the suspicion of a smile.

'No, I never met anyone with that name, I'm very

sure of that. Certain. You must have your facts wrong, and you weren't born at Thorn House.'

Juliet swallowed. Was she wrong? Had her mother given her the wrong information? Could Irene's memory be faulty after all this time? Yet the names had come back to her quite easily: Birkleigh, Thorn House. Juliet looked hard at the old lady.

'I'm quite sure I'm right, Mrs Maybury. I was born at Thorn House on the same day — or night — as Donna Hazell. I can't imagine why you're refusing to acknowledge it, but there's no denying you must have been there.'

She felt rather than heard David's gasp of horror. She saw the spasm of anger that crossed Mrs Maybury's flushed features. The older woman stood up quickly, cake crumbs falling to the carpet, and faced Juliet.

'I don't know what you're accusing me of, young lady. Are you aware that you're getting perilously close to slander? I've never met an Elaine Webb, I do not remember your birth, and I'm sure I didn't deliver you!'

Juliet jumped to her feet. 'I'm sorry if I —— '

'If this is the way you repay my hospitality, then I have no wish to entertain you again.'

The next second David was on his feet, crossing to his grandmother, who was trembling uncontrollably.

'Please, Granny, don't get so upset. Juliet didn't mean to accuse you of anything — go and wait in the car, Juliet —— ' His voice was tight and controlled. 'Of course we believe you when you say you never met the girl. And it's a long time ago —— '

'There's nothing wrong with my memory, David!' The old lady sounded close to tears. 'Why did you have to bring her here? I knew as soon as I saw her she was going to be trouble!'

Juliet didn't wait to hear more. Holding back the tears, she grabbed her bag and stumbled from the house. The car was locked, and she was forced to sit on a low wall that surrounded the garden while she waited for David to return. She knew she'd made a hash of the whole thing, and she'd let her tongue run away with

her. Even so, the older woman's reactions had been a
bit over the top. What had she said? 'I knew as soon as
I saw her she was going to be trouble.' What a thing to
say to a complete stranger!

Juliet put her face in her hands. Kate Maybury had
expected trouble! And the way she'd looked at her on
the doorstep, and the cup of tea she'd spilled and
blamed on her age. Her hands had been as steady as a
rock until David mentioned Donna's birth, and Juliet's
on the same day, and Thorn House——

She sat up straight and stared into space, her eyes
wide. She'd been right! Kate Maybury did remember her
mother, and she'd probably delivered Juliet. So why was
she lying? Oh, surely David would see she was right!
He was angry with her right now, but that was because
he didn't understand, he hadn't seen what she had seen!

The door of the house opened, and she heard a few
words exchanged between David and his grandmother.
Then the door was closed and she heard his footsteps
coming down the path. She fought back the sudden urge
to run to him, to fling herself into his arms and beg his
forgiveness. She longed, at that moment, to feel his
strong arms around her, his firm lips on hers. . .

'Get in.' His voice was harsher than she'd ever heard
before. Looking suitably woebegone, she climbed into
the car.

'Well?'

She was afraid to look at him. 'I did say I was
sorry——'

'I should think you are sorry! How on earth could
you talk to an old lady like that, and my grandmother
into the bargain? You can't go around calling people
liars just because their memories are a bit faulty. Juliet,
I'm afraid you're not prepared for this search at all, you
don't know what you've got into, and I think you ought
to call it off right now. I'm not at all happy with the
way you're behaving.'

Disappointment sat like a boulder inside Juliet's
stomach. She'd ruined everything! And now David
didn't want any part of it, and she'd been so looking

forward to their sharing in the discoveries. But it wasn't entirely her fault. Mrs Maybury was definitely acting very strangely. Surely David must have seen that?

'I wish you'd let me explain.'

'I don't think there's anything to explain. You were very rude to my grandmother, and that's all there is to it. I'll take you home now.' He started the engine.

'Please, David—listen to me!' She was fighting back the tears, and her throat hurt.

'There's nothing more to say.' The car moved forward, jerkily, angrily.

'David——'

'You were unspeakably rude to someone I love dearly, and there was no excuse at all. None! I don't want to hear any more.'

Juliet sat rigidly in her seat, biting back the frustrated tears that constricted her throat. Disjointed words burst from her.

'How can you? You promised—you offered—didn't you notice anything? You must have seen——'

David's voice was unnaturally harsh. 'I saw nothing, I noticed nothing, and I have never promised anything. Now we'll say no more about it. I suggest you spend a long time thinking about what you really want.'

He was driving faster than usual, and Juliet stole a sideways glance at him. His jaw was set, and a muscle in his temple twitched. Why wouldn't he listen? Was this the end—of everything? No, dammit—and she tightened her mouth obstinately. If he won't help me, then I'll do it on my own, and he can't stop me! She could feel the adrenalin surging as she made her decision. She could do it! She didn't need Dr David Kent, who obviously couldn't see what was in front of his face.

Yet he was such a good doctor, so perceptive. Why couldn't he see what she had seen? Because he hadn't been looking? Or he had seen and couldn't believe it. His own grandmother, hiding something from them. Yes, that must be it.

How can I make him see? thought Juliet, a little

sadly. Somehow she couldn't imagine going on in her search alone. It had been so nice, so comforting, having David beside her, knowing he sympathised with what she wanted.

Perhaps he never properly understood, she thought, as the car sped along the roads to Yonder. But I really did think he did.

They didn't speak until the car reached Deerhurst Road. Juliet felt numb now, her emotions buried under a deliberate façade of nonchalance. She opened the car door.

'Thank you for bringing me home,' she said in a light voice, and David glanced briefly at her as she climbed from the car.

'Don't mention it.' His eyes seemed to be dark with emotion, and she wanted to say something, even apologise again, but he had turned away and started the car. Swallowing hard, she murmured, 'Goodbye,' and watched the Renault move swiftly away.

CHAPTER NINE

IRENE had made scones for tea. Juliet smelled them as soon as she was inside the house.

'Is that you, Doug?' Juliet pushed open the kitchen door. 'Oh, you're back early, dear. Did you have a nice day?'

'Quite nice, thank you.' Well, it had been, up to the last half-hour or so.

Irene glanced quickly at her, but didn't comment. 'I made extra scones,' she said. 'I thought you might have brought that young doctor back with you.'

'You mean David. No, he had—a prior engagement.' He could have done, Juliet told herself. Probably with someone who didn't insult his family.

'Your father's taken Domino for a walk on the common. If I know him, he'll make a detour to Bill's to talk snooker. Still, we can have ours. Did you have a nice lunch?'

'We went to a pub in Pershore.'

Irene glanced up. 'Pershore? Who lives there?'

'The ex-matron of Thorn House—the maternity home.'

'She must have met Elaine. How lucky for you. Come on, let's do it in style in the sitting-room.'

Once they were settled, Juliet said, 'No one seems to have known Elaine.'

Her mother glanced sharply at her. 'Disappointed?'

'And puzzled.' Juliet told her mother briefly of what Miss Rose had told them, but said very little about the visit to Kate Maybury, or her own suspicions of her. She couldn't help thinking, though, that the freshly baked scones reminded her of Mrs Maybury's delicious home-made cake.

'I suppose her memory's a bit faulty,' Irene commented on the old lady's assertion that she'd never seen

127

Elaine. Juliet didn't say anything, still hearing Mrs Maybury's unshakeable belief in her memory. Then her father returned, and she had to tell him the story all over again.

'It does seem strange,' he mused. 'Someone must have met her. Particularly if you were born on the same day as this other girl in the hospital.'

'Donna. Yes, it is odd. Of course, they'd remember Donna's mother because she was in labour such a long time, and they were all worried about her. Still, perhaps something will turn up.' Privately, Juliet was feeling rather despondent. If Mrs Maybury wouldn't tell them any more, what could she do? She poured herself more tea.

It was during the evening, as they were watching television, that the phone rang. Irene got up.

'I expect it's Vera — she promised to give me a recipe for salmon mousse. Tell me if I miss anything important.' It was a Ruth Rendell mystery. She went into the hall, but was back almost at once.

'It's for you, Juliet. Someone called Rose.'

'Rose? Oh — is it Miss Rose?' She rushed into the hall and picked up the receiver. 'Hello? This is Juliet Avery speaking. Miss Rose?'

'Juliet — I hope I haven't interrupted your evening. In fact, I doubted that you'd be in, thought you'd be out with that nice doctor friend of yours.'

'It's kind of you to ring, Miss Rose.' Juliet took a deep breath. 'Did you remember something?'

'Yes. I was thinking, for a long time after you left. By the way, did you find Mrs Maybury all right?'

'Yes, we did, but she couldn't remember much.'

'How very strange. Well, I don't know what she might have told you, but I racked my memory and I came up with a name. A small dark-haired girl — she looked very much like you, actually — was admitted during that Friday evening, after I went off duty. She wasn't booked with us, she was a few weeks early, and that's why I couldn't bring her to mind straight away.'

Juliet held her breath. She gripped the receiver tightly.

'If my memory is correct,' Miss Rose went on, 'she delivered very soon after Mrs Hazell. I remember now Mrs Maybury grumbling because she'd had to do it all herself. The relief nurse was late arriving.'

Juliet still said nothing. Her skin seemed to be tingling.

'I don't think it's going to help you much,' said Miss Rose. 'I doubt if she was your mother.'

Juliet swallowed. 'Why not? What was her name?'

'Parsons. Lilian Parsons.'

Juliet's shoulders sagged. 'But you said she was a small, dark-haired girl, looked like me.'

'Oh, yes, she did, very much like you. In fact, I think it was seeing you, there on the doorstep, that jogged my memory. But that isn't all.'

Juliet's throat felt dry. 'Oh,' she croaked.

'She had twins, a boy and a girl. Mrs Maybury delivered them, but the second one, the boy, was stillborn. So you see, it doesn't seem likely she could have been your mother. You'd have known that, wouldn't you, that you'd been a twin?'

'Yes, I suppose I would. Miss Rose, was she a widow? Do you remember?'

'A widow? Oh, no, as far as I can recall, she was a single girl. Mrs Maybury was quite scathing about it, but she is a little old-fashioned, and times have changed. I quite liked the girl — Lily, she was called.'

'I see. Well, thank you for taking the trouble to ring me, Miss Rose.'

'That's all right. I hope you find her. I'll tell you something, Juliet. If Lily *had* been your mother, I just can't imagine her ever giving you up.'

Juliet replaced the receiver and stood looking at it. Twins, a boy and a girl. Lilian Parsons. Anything? Or nothing? She walked slowly back to the sitting-room.

'All right, dear?' asked her mother, keeping her gaze on the television screen. Inspector Wexford had just revealed the murderer.

'Mother, I don't like to keep dragging this up, but did Elaine ever tell you I was a surviving twin?'

The credits were rolling. Irene turned the sound down and turned to her daughter. 'What was that? A twin? Elaine had twins?'

'I don't know. Someone had twins that night, a girl who looked a lot like me. One of them was stillborn — a boy. But the girl's name wasn't Elaine Webb.'

'But what a coincidence. No, Elaine never mentioned anything to me about your being a twin.'

'Perhaps she realised that something like that would make it easier for her to be found.'

'So you're assuming this girl was Elaine?' put in her father.

'I don't want to assume anything. This other girl was named Lilian Parsons. But this could just be one big red herring. Elaine could have delivered the night before — after midnight, to have the same date of birth — and perhaps Mrs Maybury wasn't on duty that night — and Elaine could have left the next day, so Mrs Maybury was telling the truth when she said she'd never seen her.'

'Is that likely, dear?' said Irene. 'I thought early discharges were a recent innovation.'

'It was just an idea. Elaine could have discharged herself.'

'You're forgetting something,' put in Douglas. 'Even if Elaine did come and go very quickly, Miss Rose would have had something to do with it.'

'That's true.' Juliet slumped in her chair. 'If only Elaine had got round to registering the birth! She'd have had to say it was twins, if it had been, wouldn't she? And it would have shown on the certificate, the time of birth — it's only done for multiple births. Sister on Rainbow told me. So now I shall never know, because no one would have thought about twins when I was found. And I suppose I was registered by the social worker as a single.'

'I suppose so,' said Irene. 'We've only got your adoption certificate.'

'Oh, why don't people want to help me?' wailed Juliet in frustration, thinking of Mrs Maybury, but really meaning David Kent.

'I did warn you, dear,' said Irene. 'I told you you'd be disappointed.'

David had said the same sort of thing, thought Juliet, and a deep feeling of sadness washed over her. As soon as Miss Rose had rung, her first thought had been, Wait until I tell David! Now it didn't matter. He wouldn't be interested.

'I'm going to bed,' she said, getting up and kissing her parents. 'I'm very tired.

'I thought you'd be too excited to sleep,' smiled Douglas as he turned the pages of the *Radio Times*.

'No. Goodnight.'

Irene watched her anxiously as she left the room.

Juliet climbed the stairs, feeling unutterably weary. This day should have been one of the best days of her life, the start of her search. It was true, she had learned important facts from Miss Rose, although Mrs Maybury had only helped by revealing her own anxieties. She does know something! Juliet told herself stubbornly, as she climbed into bed. Her bedside clock showed ten-thirty. Miss Rose wasn't lying, so Mrs Maybury *had* to know more than she'd told them.

But how can I convince David, when he obviously doesn't want to see me again? she thought. All her discoveries seemed to count for nothing if he didn't care. He did care, I'm sure he did! He cared as much as I do. She shook her head sadly. Perhaps I care too much, and it shows. Care about what? she thought sleepily. My search? Or David Kent?

Downstairs, the doorbell rang. Juliet sat up in bed. Whoever could it be at this time of night? The front door was opened, and she heard her father's low voice, then another one that sounded like—— A tide of colour suffused her cheeks. David?

Her father called up the stairs. 'Juliet? David's here. He wants a word with you.'

Juliet's first instinct was to hide under the blankets.

What had he come back for? He'd made it very clear
any relationship between them was over. Could she
have left something in his car? No, he'd have given it to
her at the hospital. But how can I face him again, after
this afternoon? she thought. Worse still, how can I face
him dressed like this?

'Juliet?' called her father again. 'Are you asleep? Shall
I tell him to come up?'

Instantly, Juliet was out of bed, pulling on her sky-
blue brushed cotton dressing-gown. It wasn't very glamorous, but that didn't matter.

'I'm coming!' she called, tying the belt loosely around
her waist. At the foot of the stairs, David was listening
with interest to what her father was saying, a smile on
his lips. In that instant, Juliet felt a surge of happiness
that filled her chest and almost engulfed her. Her fingers
tightened on the banister rail, as she paused in her
descent.

The two men turned and looked at her. Douglas's
expression was full of love and pride. My daughter, it
seemed to say. Isn't she lovely?

David's eyes were fixed on her with an intensity she
hadn't seen before. What did his expression say? Forgive
me for being so mean to you? Forgive me for not
listening? Or was that wishful thinking? There was
something more in his eyes, something more than
apology.

She reached the hall. She was aware of David's
admiring gaze as it travelled over her slim body, her
firm breasts and shapely hips, and she was afraid to
look at him.

'David says you have some unfinished business,' said
her father. 'I expect it's private, so perhaps you'd like to
go into the dining-room? Or the kitchen? You could
make yourselves a drink.'

Trying to hide her enormous delight in his return,
Juliet turned to David. 'Will cocoa do?' she asked
lightly.

'I take it it's the kitchen, then?' he said, following her
along the short hall.

Douglas went back to the sitting-room, and Juliet heard him say, 'It's David. He wants to ——' The door closed behind him.

Juliet poured milk into a saucepan. This is ludicrous! she was thinking. What am I doing, entertaining David Kent in my dressing-gown? David was seated, his elbows on the table, watching her.

'I know I'm six hours too late,' he said in a low voice. 'And it's been six hours of torment for me. I expect you ——' He broke off. Juliet tensed as she spooned drinking chocolate into two mugs. She couldn't answer. What did he want her to say?

'Is it too late, Juliet?' The tenderness in his voice caused a sob to rise in her throat.

'I don't know,' she whispered. Her hands trembled as she poured the milk into the mugs.

'Come here.' His voice was soft but still held authority. She was trying desperately to regain her composure. It was difficult, trying to appear dignified in an old dressing-gown.

'I'm making the cocoa!'

'Damn the cocoa.' She heard his chair scrape, and then his arm was on her shoulder, gently but firmly turning her to face him. He sighed, and softly wiped away a single tear with the tip of his finger.

'I should kiss you here, but that would ruin all my resolutions, so it will have to wait. We have to talk. And this time I promise to listen to you.'

He placed the mugs of cocoa on the table, and they sat near to each other, Juliet sure she was still in bed and dreaming. David reached out and took her hand, pressing her fingertips to his lips.

'I know how much all this means to you, finding Elaine. I've been through it all before, and I felt sure you were going to get hurt. Perhaps that was why I was so angry, because it seemed to be going that way. Perhaps I was trying to stop you. I realise now, I don't have the right. Do you understand?'

'I'm not sure. But you had every right to be angry with me. I was very rude and tactless with your grandmother. I couldn't help it. I'm too—impulsive, I'm afraid.'

'I'm not sorry for being angry over that,' he said, surprisingly. 'Yes, you were rude. My apology is for not listening to you when you tried to explain.'

Juliet didn't answer. She was aware of the mugs of cocoa, cooling on the table beside her, but she only wanted to prolong this wonderful moment, sitting here with David, her hand in his. I think I might be falling in love, the words kept running through her brain. Is this what it's like? And her heart seemed to quicken in response.

'Do you want to tell me now?' He released her hand, lifting her chin with his finger, his gaze moving over her face, finally meeting her own. Almost as though he's trying to memorise what I look like, thought Juliet, knowing she could never forget his brown eyes and curling eyelashes, and the smile that hovered on his lips.

'Will you listen this time?'

'I've already promised this time I'll listen.' He watched her attentively, feigning deep concentration. Juliet had to smile.

'You're laughing at me! I shan't tell you unless you're serious.'

'Believe me, Juliet, I'm deadly serious.' He sat back in his chair and crossed his legs. He was still wearing the same clothes he'd worn that afternoon, and Juliet wondered if he had been out that evening, and who with.

'First of all, I'm sure your grandmother knows something about Elaine,' she began. She glanced at him. He shrugged.

'Carry on. However outrageous, I'm prepared to listen.'

'As soon as she saw me on the doorstep I felt she knew something. It wasn't just a hunch—I saw her expression change. And then you mentioned Thorn House, and my birth on the same day as Donna, and she was so shocked she spilled her tea. And the strangest thing of all—and I'm sure you noticed it too—she

denied delivering me even before she knew who my
mother was.'

David sighed. 'Yes, I have to admit, I did notice that.
It was a strange reaction. And, if you recall, I asked
how she could be so sure. She didn't answer.'

'Yes, and she was so vehement about my looking for
Elaine. Why should it mean anything to her? Yet she
was quite aggressive about it.'

David nodded. 'It worries me. I've never seen her so
upset before. What have you stirred up, Juliet?'

'I just want information about Elaine, that's all, and
I'm sure your grandmother knows something. But why
didn't Elaine's name mean anything to her? She was
telling the truth there—I watched her reaction.'

'Yet you still accused her of lying——'

'I didn't! Not in so many words. All right, my tongue
ran away with me. I suppose it was a shock to her, that
we'd talked to Miss Rose, and heard about Celia and
Donna. I don't think it's unethical for an aunt to deliver
her niece's baby.'

'It isn't,' David put in. 'It's accepted that doctors
don't look after their own families. And I think in some
hospitals they're not keen for the midwife and mother to
know each other personally. But that's usually waived,
if the mother agrees. I'm sure it must be comforting for
the mother to have someone she knows well helping
her.'

'That's what's so puzzling,' said Juliet. 'If it's not
unethical—and there was no one else to do it, anyway—
why have Celia and your grandmother kept it secret all
these years? What was so wrong about it?'

'Nothing wrong, I'm sure. I think perhaps my grandmother felt it to be unethical, that's all. Probably told
Celia it was too. Nothing mysterious.'

Juliet didn't answer, but frowned speculatively at her
mug of cocoa. David drank, watching her.

'There is something mysterious,' Juliet said finally.
'Miss Rose rang this evening.'

David's eyes widened. 'What did she have to say?'

'Quite a lot.' She told him what the old lady had said. David looked amazed.

'Lilian Parsons? Twins? But it doesn't make sense. Why should she tell your mother her name was Elaine Webb?'

'Well, that's obvious. She'd have to use her real name to have the baby, because of the records and things. But later, when she didn't want to be traced, she told my mother she was Elaine Webb. And everyone would be looking for Elaine Webb, who had had only one baby, not Lilian Parsons, who was in the records of Thorn House, and had had twins. Who could possibly make the connection? No one.'

David shrugged. 'You're probably right. It makes sense. So we're looking for Lilian Parsons, not Elaine Webb?' Juliet noticed he'd said 'we'. It made her feel happy.

'I think so.'

'So you were right when you said my grandmother hadn't met Elaine Webb.'

'The name meant nothing—it wouldn't. Now if I'd mentioned Lilian Parsons. . .' Juliet looked at David, who nodded slowly but said nothing. Juliet suddenly thought of something else.

'Don't you think it's surprising that she couldn't recall delivering twins for Lilian, when it happened at the same time as Donna, almost? One would think something like that would stand out in her mind.'

David frowned. 'You're not still trying to accuse her of something underhand, are you?'

Juliet knew she had to be tactful. 'I don't think underhand is the word I would choose, David. I think, rather as you did earlier, she feels I may be better off not knowing everything. And perhaps what she does know won't help me, anyway. I don't know.'

David finished his cocoa and laid down his mug. 'Did you really imagine it would be easy?'

'I didn't realise I'd be going round treading on people's corns to get at the truth!'

He laughed and stood up. 'I'm keeping you from your beauty sleep. Not that you need it.'

Juliet got to her feet. Her eyes were almost level with his mouth. She did so want him to kiss her.

'I never thanked you for taking me out today,' she said quietly, looking up at him. 'I'm sorry I nearly made a mess of things.'

'I wish I could take you out tomorrow, but I'm working. And I'm sure you need to study. Juliet, has that Westwood fellow been in touch? I know it's none of my business, but I don't want you falling for his charm again. He's too worldly-wise. He'd corrupt you.'

Juliet laughed. 'Oh, David, what do you think I am?'

'A very young, naïve, sensitive, and beautiful leprechaun.' He gazed into her eyes. 'And I just can't resist kissing leprechauns.'

He drew her to him, and she went gladly. His mouth was on hers, and her own lips were responding, and a delicious tingle seemed to be spreading from her toes to her head, and a throbbing was beginning, deep inside her.

At some point she tried to say, 'David——' but his mouth was on hers again, and his long sensitive hands were sensuously caressing her, and she never wanted it to stop.

He slowly released her, looking deep into her eyes. 'The colour of the sea,' he murmured, and his voice was husky with emotion. His eyes had a smouldering look in them, and she felt she was being hypnotised. Her heart was galloping so fast that she felt quite giddy with happiness.

He gently pushed back a strand of her inky black hair. 'I just thought I'd better warn you.' His voice was so low she could hardly hear him. 'If anyone's going to corrupt you, it's going to be me.'

'I'm sure you're not corrupt,' Juliet managed to murmur.

'But you don't know me at all, do you? I may be downright wicked. I may be warning you off that Nigel fellow, but I may be worse. Would you still let me kiss you?'

The tingling just wouldn't go away. She felt breathless. 'Oh, yes, yes!'

'And there I thought you were young and innocent!' David laughed, but the glow between them refused to die away.

Juliet leaned against his broad chest. 'This is nice,' she said. 'I wish you didn't have to go home.'

He put on an expression of mock horror. 'What are you suggesting, you Jezebel? Whatever would your parents think? They'd have me out on my nose!'

'And it's such a nice nose,' murmured Juliet, standing on tiptoe to kiss it. 'You know I didn't mean that ——'

'Didn't you? Pity.'

'I just wish you could stay longer.'

'So do I. But some people have to work tomorrow.' He stroked her cheek gently with his finger. 'Thanks for the cocoa. And the chat. And — everything else.' They walked slowly to the front door. 'Goodnight, sweet leprechaun.'

He kissed her softly on the lips, then he was walking swiftly down the path. The car door slammed, and he was gone. Juliet stood in the porch, her finger to her lips, still feeling that last, tender kiss.

Monday stretched before her like a lifetime. Although she loved her work, never before had she wished to be on duty on a day off. But she couldn't stop thinking of David in his white coat, visiting the patients, touching them, and this was where her thoughts made her tingle all over, and she had to set her mind to something else.

Is this love? she asked herself. Behaving like an infatuated teenager, just because he's taken me out, and kissed me a few times? That first kiss, in the car after Nigel's party — purely out of pity. And last night? Well, that was because — but, try as she could, there seemed to be no other reason except that he wanted to. Kisses don't mean anything these days, she thought. Everyone's doing it, all the time. She began to think of Donna instead, the photograph of the little dark-haired baby, sitting on her mother's knee at the seaside, and Celia eating an ice-cream, worried about —— She jumped up. Celia! The tissue-typing results!

'Be careful, Juliet!' her mother admonished her. 'We very nearly had a marmalade tablecloth then!' The rebuke was mildly made, and Juliet reflected on how much more tolerant her mother was lately.

'Sorry, Mum, I just thought of something. I have to make a phone call, but —— ' she glanced at the kitchen clock, ' — I think it's a bit too early.'

'To David?' smiled her mother.

'Oh — no —— ' She felt awkward. Had she been revealing her feelings about David without being aware of it? She'd have to be careful. 'I may go into Tewkesbury this afternoon, Mum. Do you need anything?'

'Tewkesbury? No, I don't think so. I usually shop on Wednesdays. I go to the market. Who are you going to see in Tewkesbury?'

'Donna's mother.' Juliet glanced at her mother, but Irene didn't pursue it further, and buttered another slice of toast.

Juliet sat on her bed, wondering how she could get hold of the tissue-typing results — if they'd come — without anyone being aware of who she was. She had no reason herself to ask for them. But Sister and some of the other nurses would know she wasn't Celia, by her voice. If she could ring when Sister wasn't likely to answer — during a consultant's round — yes, that was it! She could pretend to be Celia, say she was unable to visit. A junior nurse would probably believe her. She decided to wait until eleven o'clock, when the medical rounds were usually done. She watched the clock hands go round. While her mother was busy ironing in the kitchen, she slipped into the hall and dialled. She was put straight through to Melrose. Her heart was thudding.

'Melrose Ward, Nurse Elmore speaking.' Thank goodness it wasn't Sister!

Juliet lowered her voice a tone. 'This is Mrs Hazell,

Donna's mother. Can you tell me if the tissue-typing
results are back yet?'

'Tissue-typing? Oh, hell, I haven't the faintest!' Just
like Frankie Elmore, thought Juliet. 'Wait a minute, I'll
find out for you.' Piece of cake, thought Juliet. She
hasn't recognised my voice. I should have been an
actress. She could hear conversation in the distance, and
Sister's voice — oh, no, Sister would be suspicious —

'Just a minute, Mrs Hazell.' Frankie again. 'I think
you may have to wait until you come to visit Donna.
Did they tell you to ring today? Because I think it's a
bit early — oh — '

'David Kent here. Can I help you, Celia?'

Juliet felt blood rushing into her ears. For a moment
she couldn't speak. Should she admit her ruse, or could
she — no. She spoke boldly, in her own voice.

'David! How nice. This is Juliet. Sorry to ring when
you're busy.'

'I was told it was Celia. What's going on?'

'Oh, I think Nurse Elmore must have misunderstood.
I thought of going to see Celia, and then I thought
she might be at the hospital, for the tissue-typing
results — '

'They haven't come yet, Juliet. It's too soon. And
Celia will be at school anyway, so she can't visit until
tonight.'

There was an awkward pause. Juliet wondered if he
was suspicious of her excuse. But she had learned what
she'd rung for.

'I forgot about that, David. Such a lot on my mind
since yesterday.'

His voice softened. 'Same here. But why do you want
to see Celia? I hope you don't intend to upset her —
we've had enough of that. Tact isn't your strongest
point, is it?' His voice lowered. 'But it's a very endearing
habit.'

'I shan't upset her, David. But she was at Thorn
House the same time as Elaine, and she must have
spoken to her. I can't think why it didn't occur to me
before.'

'I understand that, Juliet. But you will be careful, won't you? For me?'

'I'll be the soul of discretion for you, David.'

'Good girl. Don't forget, she won't be home until about four o'clock.' His voice had grown low and confidential. Juliet visualised him standing in Sister's office, his soft brown eyes concerned and tender, his curly brown hair a bit ruffled, a smile at the corner of his mouth. And broad shoulders under his white coat — She could feel her hand trembling.

'It is number 52, isn't it?' she asked, just to keep him at the end of the line.

'That's right. But I have to go now. I'll see you tomorrow. Looking forward to it.'

She replaced the receiver, her eyes bright. He did like her, he did! He didn't have to say those last few words. He could have just said goodbye. She could hardly wait until tomorrow! But there was no point in mooning around until then. Here was one investigation she could do on her own. Find out if Celia Hazell had talked to Elaine, and, just as important, try to find out why she was so terrified of the tissue-typing results.

The bus from Yonder to Tewkesbury ran every twenty minutes. Juliet had looked on the street map, and worked out that the nearest bus stop in Tewkesbury would be the Crescent. From there, it shouldn't take more than ten minutes, past the Abbey and the cemetery, to Barley Hill, just off the Gloucester Road.

The sky was darkening, and no breeze disturbing the trees, so Juliet slipped on her red raincoat over her jeans and cream shirt. Irene was resting upstairs. She called to her to say she'd be back for tea, and went out to catch the bus.

It began to rain when she was halfway along Gloucester Road, big spots like buttons hitting the pavement. She scurried around the corner into Barley Hill, but by the time she reached number 52 her hair was glistening with raindrops. She stood in the porch and rang the bell. It was a smart house, semi-detached

like their own, but larger, more modern. She glanced at
her watch, hoping she wasn't too early. Four-twenty.
She rang again. Then she heard the distinctive sounds
of a loquacious Siamese cat, and a human voice raised
in exasperation.

'Persephone, will you please get from under my feet?
You can't have more tuna!'

The door opened. Celia Hazell, looking more attractive in a loose, flowered dress than the peach suit, stared
at Juliet for a while, puzzled. Then her brow cleared.

'You're the nurse on Donna's ward — I recognise you.
Well, you'd better come in. You know, when I said let
me know about the blood results, I didn't expect you to
call in person.' She gave a short laugh, then looked
intensely at her. 'Have they come, then?'

Juliet followed her into the house, and the cat purred
loudly, rubbing against her legs. She bent and stroked
it.

'Actually, Mrs Hazell, that isn't why I'm here.'

Celia looked alarmed. 'Is something wrong? Donna?
Oh, of course not — they wouldn't send you, they'd
phone. Come in and sit down. Sorry about the mess,
but I'm not long back from school. Those second-years!
It must be the most difficult age ever invented!'

They both laughed, and settled themselves in the
open-plan sitting-room. The furniture wasn't new, but
had been expensive: a good leather suite and real yew
furniture. Juliet felt tense. She sat on the edge of her
chair.

'I don't really know how to put this, Mrs Hazell.
What I'm looking for is information about myself. And
my mother.'

Celia frowned. 'I don't understand. Why come to
me?'

'I was adopted, you see. And I was born at Thorn
House in Birkleigh.'

There was no answering response from Celia. She too
sat rigidly in her chair. Juliet could see her white
knuckles.

'Donna was born at Thorn House, wasn't she?' prompted Juliet.

Celia nodded. She licked her lips. 'That's right. It was a dreadful time. I don't like to be reminded of it.'

Juliet nodded sympathetically. 'I met Miss Rose, the ex-matron of Thorn House. She told me you had a very difficult time.'

'Forty-two hours in labour. I was exhausted. And the baby.'

'She showed me a photograph you sent her — you and Donna.'

Celia laughed. She seemed more relaxed now. 'That's right. We had an Indian summer that year, very warm until October, I think. We went to Weston-super-Mare for a few days. Donna had been too small to travel before then.'

'She was born on April the tenth, wasn't she?'

'Yes — a Friday. I was only glad it was all over. The midwife —— ' here she hesitated ' — was very worried, and sent for the doctor to do a forceps delivery. But he was out at a coronary, I believe, and by the time he arrived the baby was born.'

'Your aunt was the midwife, wasn't she?'

A closed look came over Celia's face.

'Did she tell you? She shouldn't have done. It wasn't ethical, you see. Family. She told me to keep it quiet.'

'I don't think she did anything wrong, Mrs Hazell,' said Juliet softly. 'After all, she was the only one there, wasn't she? And your aunt didn't tell me, it was Miss Rose. She didn't seem to think it was a crime.'

'No. Perhaps you're right, Nurse — Avery, isn't it?'

'Please call me Juliet. Donna and I have become quite friendly, and if I call here to see her you can't really call me Nurse.'

Celia smiled. 'I'm Celia. Now, you've been talking about Donna's birth, but I thought it was your own you wanted to find out about?'

'I thought you might have met my mother, talked to her. I'm hoping she might have said something to someone which might help me find her.'

'I don't think I met anyone who was having her baby adopted. I'd have remembered something like that.'

'I don't think she intended to have me adopted at that time. All I know is she looked a lot like me, and gave birth to me the same day as Donna.'

For a moment Celia looked disconcerted. She bit her lip, and played with a button on the chair.

'What was her name?'

'I thought it was Elaine Webb, but now I'm not so sure. I'll be honest with you, Celia: it wasn't an ordinary adoption. She left me with my adoptive mother and just disappeared. And I'm beginning to think she gave my mother an assumed name.'

'There was no one called Elaine at Thorn House while I was there. I would have known, because all the postnatal mothers were in one ward. It was only a small place, not many deliveries. I think they closed it down a few years later. There was Riverside, you see, at Yonder — ' Celia broke off and gave Juliet a vague smile.

'Do you remember any other mothers who delivered on April the tenth, Celia? Before or after you?'

Celia screwed up her face in an effort to think back. 'There was Diane, I got quite friendly with Diane. She had a boy — oh, no, she was the day before, and Anne — no, she was the day after — it's very difficult — '

'You don't remember the small dark girl who had her baby only minutes after you, that your aunt also delivered?'

For only a second, a terrified look crossed Celia's plain face, then she laughed. 'You mean Lilian? Of course, how could I forget her? Yes, you're quite right, she delivered very quickly, just after she arrived. I suppose that's why I forgot her.'

Juliet's pulses were racing. 'Did you talk to her? Did she talk to you?'

'Not much. She was a single girl, did you know that? She didn't talk much to anyone. She was upset. One of her babies — Look, I don't really have time to talk, I have a meal to prepare——' Celia stood up. Juliet reluctantly followed suit.

'Yes, she had twins, didn't she?' she asked Celia. 'A girl and a boy, and the boy was stillborn. Am I right?'

'If you know so much, why are you asking me?'

'Because that's all I do know, and I'm looking for evidence that I'm the surviving twin.'

Celia stared at her intently, a strange look in her eyes. 'Yes—yes,' she muttered, 'I'm sure you are.' Then she smiled. 'Now I really must get on. When do you think the blood results will come through?'

'We're hoping tomorrow. There's no rush.' Juliet took the bull by the horns. 'Celia, you seem very worried about it. Why? Can you tell me?'

'No! I mean—I'm not at all worried. Only about Donna, of course. I am her mother, so naturally I'm concerned to find a perfect match. You see, Juliet, I know my blood-group isn't the same as Donna's——'

'The blood-groups aren't so important in bone-marrow transplants,' Juliet reminded her.

'No—you said. But you will still ring me? Just to let me know who's a good match? You can ring me at school; this is the number.' Celia scribbled on a post-card. 'Then I can tell Alan. I think it would be better if I told Alan the bad news. Or the good news,' she added quickly. 'He doesn't understand all the technicalities.'

'I'll certainly do that, Celia.'

Celia ushered her to the door. 'It was so nice of you to come and see me. Another time I shall have more time to offer you some tea. But at least we now understand each other.'

She closed the door quickly, and Juliet stood on the porch, slightly bemused by the way things had gone. David would be pleased, anyway, because she hadn't upset Celia.

The rain had nearly stopped, so she hurried back up the Gloucester Road for her bus. And on the bus she couldn't help thinking about what Celia had said. 'It would be better if I told Alan the bad news.' She was expecting bad news! Juliet began to feel quite excited inside. She had such a lot to tell David tomorrow! She could hardly wait!

She watched the houses go past. It was very strange. Both Mrs Maybury and her niece, Celia, gave the impression that they knew a lot more than they were admitting. Was it to do with Donna? Or herself? I should have been a detective, she thought, as her journey ended. I'm getting hooked on this!

CHAPTER TEN

THE routine on Melrose Ward had barely been established next morning, when Casualty rang to say they were sending up a woman with jaundice who had collapsed in the street. Juliet and Sara Calvert were sent to get a bed ready.

'I hope she's not infectious,' said Sara, as they rearranged the sheets for admission.

'Why should she be?'

'Jaundice. Could be hepatitis. I'm surprised Sister didn't ask for a single room. Now Bobbie Cole's in H, we've got G free.'

'They must have decided in Cas that she isn't hepatitis,' said Juliet.

Sara shrugged. 'Not for us to wonder why. There, that's done.'

As they turned to leave the porters arrived, Sister following the stretcher with the patient's folder in her hand. The patient was helped on to the bed, and the porters left. Sister drew the curtains.

The woman looked around middle age — although, according to the notes, she was only thirty-eight — very thin, except for a grossly enlarged abdomen, and her yellowish hair was stringy and uncombed. Her clothes looked like jumble-sale rejects, and she smelled — of dirt, sweat, ammonia and alcohol.

'A genuine bag lady,' murmured Sara, and Sister glared at her.

'Whatever this patient's origins or inclinations, she is entitled to the same care and respect we give to all the others on the ward. Please remember that, Nurse Calvert. This could be you one day. Now I suggest you go and help Mrs Forrest to the bath, while we deal with Mrs Toye.'

147

Sara looked sulky and left them to it, and they heard her calling to the old lady with rheumatoid arthritis.

'Fetch a bowl of hot water, Nurse Avery. We can't leave her in this state for the doctor to examine!'

Shades of Hayley Burton, thought Juliet, as she obeyed. She was soon back with a trolley and all the necessary requisites, and between them they washed the woman from top to toe, and dressed her in a white hospital gown. With her hair combed, she began to look more human.

'That's better, Sylvia,' said Sister cheerfully. Mrs Toye stared at her and a strange smile spread across her face. Her teeth badly needed treatment.

'Watcher, Madge! Gotta fag on yer?'

'I'm sorry, I haven't.'

'Ne'er mind. Got the price of a drink?'

'Not now. The doctor's coming to see you. You collapsed in the street.'

'The street? Where?'

Sister sighed. 'Outside the Rose and Crown.'

'Did I?' The woman turned and stared at Juliet. 'Bit of 'er doin', I expect. Won't leave my chap alone. Yer know what you are, don't yer?'

Juliet was taken aback. 'I'm a nurse —'

'Ha! Nurse!' Without warning, the woman's hand flew out, striking Juliet on the shoulder and causing her to lose her balance. She tried to catch the bed, but missed it and fell heavily to the floor.

'Nure Avery!' Sister moved quickly, but it was other hands that helped her to her feet, strong male hands.

'Are you hurt?' David's brown eyes looked anxiously into hers.

'No — no, I just lost my balance.' Her heart was racing.

'You're breathless — a bit shocked. You'd better sit down.' He pulled a low seat from under the bed and gently eased her down to it. Juliet felt embarrassed. How could she tell him she wasn't shocked at all; she was breathless because of his proximity?

'I'm really all right,' she insisted, getting up again, 'just surprised. Mrs Toye mistook me for someone else.'

'Thinks I'm Madge,' smiled Sister. 'I hope she likes you, Dr Kent. If you're all right, Nurse Avery, you can stay while the doctor looks at Mrs Toye. Dr Whitfield is coming to see Bobbie Cole.'

'You can't keep him waiting, Sister,' said David, as Sister left the bedside. He turned towards Sylvia Toye, who was watching him with a smile on her face.

'Who do you think I am?' he asked.

She grinned. 'What a daft question. You're the doctor. You've got a white coat on.'

With that problem out of the way, he carefully examined her, frowning at the obvious ascites in her abdomen.

'The perils of drink,' he murmured to Juliet, as he tucked away his stethoscope.

Mrs Toye heard him. 'What did you say, Doc? You gotta drink?'

'No, and you can't have any either. You realise it's slowly killing you?'

'They said that last time I was in, but I'm still 'ere, ain't I?'

David sighed. He began to write up his findings in the notes. Juliet poured a glass of water, and handed it to Mrs Toye. The woman's eyes widened as she took it, but at the first taste she thrust it at Juliet, pulling a face.

'Tryin' to fool me, are yer? Just like you, Deirdre Watkins!'

'My name is Juliet Avery,' Juliet explained patiently. 'I'm a nurse.'

'Where's yer apron, then?'

'We don't wear aprons now.'

David came and stood at her shoulder, smiling at her attempts to convince Mrs Toye. 'Come to the office and I'll tell you what I want done. See you later, Sylvia.'

'Wanna go home.'

'She hasn't got a home,' said David, as they walked together across the ward. 'This is the fourth time she's

been in, apparently. It seems we have a job getting rid
of her!'

In the office he stood very close to her, pointing out
what he'd written.

'Just in case you can't read my handwriting,' he said,
adding softly, 'I missed you yesterday, did you see
Celia?'

'Yes. She said——' He put a finger to his lips.

'Not here. When are you off duty?'

'I've got a split shift. But I shan't go home this
afternoon, there won't be time.'

'I'll see you down at the river at three o'clock. Take
your study books with you. By the willow. Then we can
talk.'

'All right.'

'Now, to Sylvia Toye. You probably realised she's a
severe case of portal cirrhosis, with ascites and jaundice.
Her brain's affected too, unfortunately. Not much we
can do, unless she stops drinking. We can't reverse the
process, but we might be able to check it. And we might
as well ask pigs to fly.'

'Poor Sylvia.'

David stared at her. 'You're amazing. She swipes
you, and you call her poor Sylvia.'

'She didn't know what she was doing. Well, she did,
but she thought I was someone else. Do carry on.'

'I'm going to organise a liver biopsy, liver scan, and
oesophagoscopy, in case she has varices. I want you to
organise full blood analysis, and the usual urine tests. I
want the dietician to see her. Bed rest for the moment.
Extra vitamins, especially B. And I think the medical
social worker, once she's over her present hangover.
Sylvia, that is, not the MSW.'

Juliet laughed, as she imagined the tweedy Miss
Gater having a hangover. David grinned. 'I like to see
you smile.' She thought he was going to kiss her, but it
didn't happen, because the door was pushed open and
the clerk came in with a pile of reports from other
departments.

'Ah——' David began, but, before he could look at

them, Sister had come in and picked them up. She
began to sort them into piles.

'How's our Sylvia, then?' she asked David, without
looking up.

David laid the file on the desk. 'Still cheating fate.
I've filled in and signed all the appropriate forms. Her
liver's failing, of course. We may have to consider
paracentesis this time. See what his lordship's got to say
when he comes round tomorrow.'

Sister nodded, glancing at the reports as she sorted
them. 'Biochemistry, I see Mrs Hayman's cholesterol
has gone down a bit — Lizzie's chest X-ray — haematology, Betty's haemoglobin's not too good — oh, the Hazell
family's tissue-typing results — ' She gazed at them
shaking her head sadly. 'You'd better have them, Dr
Kent. They're not very optimistic, I'm afraid.'

He took the papers, reading them. He stopped, frowning. 'But they must have made a mistake — that can't
possibly be right!'

'I'm afraid it is,' said Sister. 'No good matches at all,
I'm afraid. It happens. Have you thought of autologous
bone marrow?'

'Oh, yes,' he said, rather absently. He gave the reports
to Juliet.

'File them for me, Nurse Avery. Now I suppose I
shall have the difficult task of telling Donna. Poor kid!'
He left the office, and his footsteps gradually faded
away.

Juliet went slowly along to the nurses' station, where
the trolley of files was kept. She didn't envy David his
task. She knew how Donna had been banking on one of
the boys being a good match, and it seemed neither of
them were. Just as Celia had suspected. She stopped
dead in her tracks. Celia had expected this. How had
she known?

She laid the reports on the table and compared them.
Name, address, date of birth. Nothing wrong there.
What had David seen? She studied the blood groups.
Celia had been worried about the blood-groups. Juliet's
pulses quickened. She knew Donna was AB-negative.

Celia was O-positive. Alan was A-negative. Nothing wrong so far. Positives could pass on a negative gene. Jamie was O-positive, Gary was O-negative. So what was wrong?

Then she saw it. Where had Donna received her B antigen? Alan was A. That could have contributed to the AB. But Celia was O. No way could she pass on A or B.

Juliet sat down and pushed the papers together. This was what David must have seen. What had Celia said just before Juliet had left her house? 'Alan doesn't understand the technicalities.' Could it be he understood them too well, and would know what the discrepancy meant? Because, as far as Juliet could see, there were two ways in which Donna could have received her AB blood group. Either Celia was her mother, but her father wasn't Alan. Or Alan was her father, and Celia not her mother. Yet hadn't Celia told her about her prolonged labour, and how her aunt had saved the baby by resuscitation? Did Alan know he wasn't Donna's father?

Oh, dear, what an embarrassing state of affairs, thought Juliet, as she filed them away. It was only much later, when she was checking the dispensary, that an alternative came to mind. Much less embarrassing for Celia and Alan, but possibly a shock for Donna. Yet it explained a number of things. Except Celia's anxiety about telling Alan.

The rest of the morning went quickly. There had been lots of problems, and they were rushed off their feet. Hayley's real father had turned up, demanding to take her home with him, and there were tears and tantrums from Hayley, who declared, as she frequently did, that she'd throw herself out of the window. Miss Gater had turned up, expecting to see Sylvia Toye, but was roped in to discuss Hayley's problem.

Sylvia had started to hallucinate, seeing creepy-crawlies on her bed, and the houseman had to come and sort her out. Then the diabetic had suffered a hypoglycaemic attack. It wasn't until Juliet was sent to lunch that she remembered her rendezvous with David at three o'clock. Little chills ran up and down her spine, as she waited in the queue for her lunch. Silly, she kept telling herself. He only wants to talk.

She dawdled over her lunch, spinning out the minutes until she would see him. Later, while she was crossing the foyer of the hospital, she stopped to admire the colourful blooms on the flower stall just inside the door — carnations, pyrethrums, freesias and anemones. She stopped to sniff the freesias. And roses, all colours. She gazed at the vivid scarlet variety. A visitor paused, and picked up a selection bouquet. She reminded Juliet of Celia. But Celia was at school, teaching.

Horrified, Juliet realised she'd almost forgotten to ring her! Where was that piece of paper with the phone numbers on it? She found it in her pocket, and hurried to the nearest public telephone.

They fetched Celia from class, and Juliet felt guilty. 'I'm sorry, I've been very busy today — ' she began.

'Doesn't matter,' said Celia. 'You have the results?'

'Yes. I'm sorry, Celia, it's not good.'

'No one matches?'

'No one. I'm awfully — '

'It's not your fault. I almost expected it. Donna is — so very different from the rest of us. Nurse Avery — Juliet — did you see all the details on the forms? The — blood-groups — and things?'

'I did.'

'Has David seen them?'

'Yes.'

'Oh, God! Look — could I talk to you? Could you make Friday morning?'

'I could come early. I have a morning off.'

'You see, there's something I have to sort out. I'm not the sort of person you think I am.'

'I'm sure you're not. And I wasn't thinking anything bad about you.'

'Weren't you? After seeing those results? You're either lying or you're very naïve. Never mind. I shall tell Alan

the bad news. He doesn't need to know anything else. I
told you before, he wouldn't understand the implications, if he was told all the details. I'll see you on
Friday. Thank you for ringing.'

Juliet replaced the receiver. She was trying to put all
the pieces together. Celia had known Alan's blood-
group, and knew what it meant regarding Donna.
Perhaps Celia had been right; Alan was not aware of
what it meant, and she didn't intend that he should
know. She didn't want him asking questions.

Oh, dear, thought Juliet, as she crossed the grass
towards the river. I don't think I want to be drawn into
this web of deceit. Perhaps I shouldn't go on Friday.

The sun was warm, the grass soft beneath her san-
dalled feet. She had changed into the cotton frock she'd
worn to the hospital that morning. It was flower-
sprigged and full-skirted, snug around her trim waist,
the simple bodice emphasising her small, firm breasts.
She knew she looked good in it, and walked confidently
along. She carried a textbook on neurology in case she
had to wait long for David. She could read up Guillain-
Barré Syndrome.

There was a nice cool breeze wafting up from the
river as she settled herself in the shelter of the huge
willow tree, at the water's edge. It wasn't yet three
o'clock. She opened the book, but the susurration of the
river, the birdsong, and the distant hum of voices, made
her close her eyes. They had been very busy, she'd been
up early, and she felt sleepy.

She drifted pleasantly away, finding herself at the
theatre with Kate Maybury, but she had black hair and
carried a colander, and in the colander lay a tiny baby,
but Mrs Maybury wouldn't let her see it, just told her
to watch the show. On the stage was Moira Charles,
playing the Sleeping Beauty, and the prince looked
remarkably like David Kent. He was calling to Juliet in
the audience, telling her to wake up and watch the play.

'Come along, Sleeping Beauty, wake up.' But Moira
was the Sleeping Beauty. Mrs Maybury was now holding out the baby to her, and it was stroking her face.

'Wake up, Sleeping Beauty. Wake up, leprechaun.' A
finger was tracing the shape of her mouth. She opened
her eyes. David was sitting next to her, smiling. He
wasn't wearing his white coat.

'I hope you were having nice dreams,' he said. 'It
seemed such a shame to wake you, but I knew you'd be
really cross if you didn't get some studying done.' He
picked up the textbook from the grass. 'Oh, neurology.
I expected it to be either genetics or haematology, after
what you must have seen this morning.'

'Eh?' Juliet still felt muzzy from sleep, her mind still
full of Mrs Maybury and the colander. 'I'm not sure I
understand——'

'You're still half asleep. Perhaps this will wake you
up.' He leaned forward and kissed her on the mouth.
She struggled to clear her mind.

'I'm awake. But you can wake me again, if you like.'
She grinned mischievously at him.

He sighed. 'Some women are never satisfied.' He
kissed her again. 'Now, my remark about haematology.
You saw the tissue-typing results? I gave them to you to
file. I expected you to look at them.'

'Yes. I did. David—there's something I ought to tell
you. After all, she must have realised you'd see the
results, and wonder about the discrepancy.'

David frowned. 'Whom are we discussing?'

'Celia. She wanted to know the results before anyone
else. She was very anxious that the blood-group differ-
ences shouldn't be discussed with Alan.'

'Oh, lor', then it's worse than I thought. I saw those
blood-groups, and I told myself that no way would Celia
cheat on Alan. But what you've just said——'

'I did have an idea about it, myself,' said Juliet. 'It
did make sense, but if Alan's in the dark then it doesn't.
I wondered if Donna—like myself—had been adopted.
But Alan would know about it, wouldn't he?'

David stared at her. 'It would certainly fit in with the
blood-group problem. But no, it can't be. Didn't Celia
tell you about the awful time she had giving birth to
Donna?'

'Yes, she did. So what do we think now? I rang her, by the way, not long ago. I wasn't sure if it was unethical, but I was only telling her what she would have discovered when she visits tonight with Alan.'

'What exactly did you tell her?'

'Only that none of them matched with Donna. She mentioned the blood-groups, wants me to go and see her on Friday. But I'm not sure I ought to get involved. It's nothing to do with me.'

'I would imagine she wanted you to tell her so that she can tell Alan, and he won't expect anyone to produce the actual tissue-typing results while they're there.' He nodded. 'Well, as the blood groups have little to do with the poor matches of HLA, I see no reason to tell Alan anything. It's Celia's problem, and it's her place to tell him if she wishes.'

Juliet looked relieved. 'I think that's what I shall tell her when I go on Friday.'

'I told Donna, by the way,' said David. 'She was very disappointed.'

'I bet she was. Poor kid. Kid—she's the same age as I am.'

David nodded. 'She is—yet I always think of her as my kid sister—because I've never had a sister, I suppose.'

'She's a bit in love with you,' murmured Juliet, hoping she wasn't giving anything away.

He laughed. 'Is she—still? When I was a teenager she used to follow me everywhere. Had a bit of a crush on me, I suppose.'

'I think that's quite understandable,' said Juliet softly. 'Don't tell her I've told you, will you? I wouldn't hurt her for the world.'

She turned to meet his gaze, and her heart was suddenly beating a tattoo in her chest, because he was looking at her again with that dark, broody expression in his eyes.

He didn't answer, but slowly drew her to him until she rested her head against his broad chest. Above the open neck of his white cotton shirt, a few dark hairs curled. Juliet stifled the urge to touch them, to feel his heart beating beneath her hand.

'You are too soft-hearted for your own good,' he murmured. 'You know that? But you're so vulnerable, so naïve. You hurtle into people's lives without thinking. For instance, what will you do if you find your mother and she rejects you again?'

His strong arms tightened around her. The drooping branches of the willow tree seemed to enclose them in its own embrace.

'I think you're all being pessimistic. Elaine didn't want to give me away — Miss Rose said so. That is, if Elaine was Lilian, and I'm sure she was. For all we know, she may even be looking for me!'

'True. But she won't need to search, will she? She knows where you are. Where she left you.'

'She may not know that. For all she knows, the social services could have given me to another family. But you're right, this is where she would look first. Perhaps she thinks I hate her for giving me up.' She spoke sadly. 'But I really think I'm getting close, David — '

'It's nice, getting close,' he muttered, and nuzzled her neck. Juliet felt a strange sort of throbbing inside her, that quickly spread like tentacles of fever through her body. Instinctively she lifted her head, and their lips met, softly at first, tasting and questing. She felt herself mould her body to his, as the pressure of his lips became more eager, his mouth hungrily imprisoning hers.

She was excitedly aware of his hand, expertly unbuttoning the front of her dress, gently slipping inside and cupping her breast. She felt her nipples harden with pleasure, and gave a soft little cry of delight. Encouraged, David pushed aside the flimsy bra, and his sensitive fingers gently kneaded the soft flesh that swelled under his touch. Juliet felt she was in another world, she felt as though she were intoxicated.

Slowly he released her, and gently covered her again. She opened her eyes and looked up at him. 'That wasn't the sort of closeness I meant,' she said, and her voice trembled.

'Wasn't it? I misunderstood you.' David's brown eyes were still dark with emotion, yet there was a smile in his voice. 'It must be those Irish eyes of yours, you leprechaun.'

He kissed her again and again, but softly, and his lips caressed her neck. 'That's enough of that, David, my lad,' he said sternly. 'Next thing you'll be carrying this nymphet off to bed, you wicked man!'

Juliet laughed. If only she could tell him how she longed for him to carry her off, but wouldn't that make him think her wanton? It wasn't as if they had some sort of relationship; he had taken her out only to help her with her search. He didn't buy her red roses. It was obviously only idle flirting on his part. Not on mine, a little voice whispered in her head.

She wondered how Moira Charles responded to his kisses. Perhaps they were more than just good friends. She wondered if he'd kissed many girls, just because they were pretty and expected it. And then she recalled the time when she'd just started her training, and one of her friends had fallen madly in love with a houseman, a rather conceited young man named Stewart. During his six-month stint on the surgical wards, the two were seen going everywhere together, and all her friends could hear wedding bells. Just as Stewart reached the end of his term at Yonder, news began to filter through of his engagement — to a nurse at Tewkesbury General. Juliet's friend had tried not to show how deeply she was hurt, but everyone knew.

Juliet decided then that it wasn't going to happen to her, and now she reaffirmed that vow. If David Kent was serious about Moira Charles — and Penny Rogers wasn't the only one to have seen them together — then I'm not going to throw myself at him.

She sighed, resting her head on his broad chest. This is so nice, she thought. And he does seem to like me, but I daren't let myself fall in love with him. Pity, because she seemed to have already done just that. And Donna, too, was a bit in love with him. Poor Donna. No one to match her bone marrow. A rare blood-group, AB-negative. Not that that mattered too much.

Juliet sat up and looked at David. 'Could I be tissue-typed?'

'Whatever for?

'For Donna's bone-marrow transplant.'

'For the register of donors you'd be welcome, but what makes you think you'll match Donna, when you're not even distantly related? I'd probably be a better match. But there again, after those blood results, perhaps not. Like you, Donna seems to be a bit of a mystery.'

'Am I such a mystery, David?' she asked teasingly.

He traced her lips with his finger. 'You, Miss Anonymous, are an enigma, a mirage, belong to no one, not really there. A forsaken little ghost.' He stroked her hair, curling the ends with his finger.

'Now you've gone all poetic again.'

'Yes. We have to find you, don't we? We have to solve your secret.'

'David, I don't have any secrets——'

'Yes, you do. You went to see Celia, but you haven't told me what she said.'

Juliet gently removed his hand from her hair. 'She told me much the same as Miss Rose. After a little nudge from me she remembered Lilian Parsons, seemed to think that I could be her surviving twin. She said Lilian didn't talk to anyone, but I'm not sure that was the complete truth. Perhaps I'm just getting paranoid.'

'Perhaps you are.' He kissed the tip of her nose. 'Come on, then, let's get this tissue-typing done. Although I can't see——'

'I'm AB-negative, like Donna.' They started to walk across the grass.

'You know it's the HLA that's most important. It *may* help, having the same blood-group. We shan't know until we let those vampires loose at you.'

'Oh. I thought you'd do it.'

'You're not a patient, or the relative of a patient. You're just an—outsider, I'm afraid. And we have the best people for that. They're taking blood all day, much better at it than I am.' David took her arm as they reached the hospital.

'Still——' murmured Juliet, and they went along to the haematology department.

David didn't appear on Melrose Ward all evening. Juliet missed him, and kept looking out for him. It was only when she went to supper that she found the reason why. A junior nurse on Folliott, the male medical ward, sat at her table, full of talk about one of their patients who had suffered an acute asthmatic attack and gone into respiratory failure, and how Dr Kent had grabbed him from the jaws of death.

Juliet smiled at her terminology. The jaws of death, indeed!

'He's fabulous, isn't he?' the girl went on. 'His first name's David—he told me. I could really go for him in a big way, but he's going steady with the staff nurse on Rainbow. Did you know? Lucky thing! He's got the most fabulous eyelashes. I couldn't help but notice.'

So did I, thought Juliet, and for once she was glad to get back to the ward. David didn't arrive, and she went off duty feeling a little bereft.

'There was a phone call for you,' said Irene, when Juliet got home. The television was on.

'Who was it? Did they say?'

'Mrs Maybury. Can you ring her back? She seemed upset. I took her number, it's on the pad.'

CHAPTER ELEVEN

JULIET dialled the number apprehensively. After the way she'd upset David's grandmother on Sunday, she would have to be extremely tactful. Irene had said Mrs Maybury still sounded upset. What on earth was wrong? The phone rang at the other end, and was answered immediately, as though she had been sitting beside it, waiting.

'Kate Maybury.'

'This is Juliet Avery, I'm sorry the call is so late——'

'Don't worry about that—the time doesn't matter. I didn't realise you might be doing a late shift, but it's imperative I see you.'

'When? I'm on duty tomorrow——'

'When is the soonest you can be here?' Mrs Maybury spoke tersely.

'I finish at five o'clock, so I could be with you by six. I'm not certain about the buses, I usually cycle——'

'I don't care how you get here. Just come.'

'Mrs Maybury, is this something to do with Lilian Parsons?'

There was a short pause, and a sound that resembled a sharp intake of breath. 'I can't discuss it over the phone. I'll see you at six o'clock tomorrow. Goodbye.'

She's still mad with me, Juliet thought, as she went back to the sitting-room. I seem to have stirred up quite a hornets' nest. I shan't enjoy this meeting at all. Then came the thought that Mrs Maybury had something vital to tell her, something which would help her to find Elaine—or Lilian; it was difficult not to think of her as Elaine. And she began to feel quite buoyed up inside.

Irene was peeling an orange. 'What was that all about?'

'She wouldn't say. She wants me to go and see her after work tomorrow.'

'You think she may have something to tell you about Elaine?'

'What else can it be? I was talking to David this afternoon, and he feels it's too much of a coincidence for me not to be Lilian Parsons's surviving twin. I'm hoping that's what Mrs Maybury is going to tell me.' She perched on the arm of a chair.

Irene looked up and smiled. 'Help yourself to an orange, Juliet. They're fresh.'

'No, I shan't bother — I'm very tired. I'll have a bath and go to bed and read for a while. Goodnight.' She kissed her mother and went upstairs. She was tired, emotionally drained. So much had happened. And she couldn't get David's kisses and caresses out of her mind.

Juliet didn't sleep well, and when she arrived on Melrose next morning it was almost as though she hadn't been away. Sister read from the Kardex the details of the patients, but Juliet found it hard to concentrate; her mind was on her visit to Mrs Maybury.

'Sylvia Toye is still hallucinating. Be careful when she swats at a fly or a spider, she may swat you by mistake. Be on your guard.' Sister glanced at Juliet. Juliet looked suitably abashed.

'Treat Hayley with kid gloves today,' Sister went on. 'She's still upset after her father's visit. I'm trying to get some counselling for her. Bobbie Cole tells us she has pins and needles in her toes — must be a good sign. Gaynor Summers is gamely attempting to knit again; she's still in some pain. Oh, and the ward clerk's away because her little boy has chickenpox, so that's more work for us, unless they can send us a replacement.'

She quickly organised tasks for the morning, and the nurses dispersed. Just before eleven o'clock, one of the consultants came to do a ward round, followed by his entourage of junior doctors and medical students. They were with Sylvia Toye for long time. David had winked at Juliet as he passed Bobbie's bed, where the physiotherapist had just finished. Juliet had looked away quickly, in case her reaction caused comment.

'He's very nice, isn't he, that Dr Kent?' said Bobbie, later. 'I'll never forget how gentle he was when I first came in.'

Juliet remembered too. It seemed a lifetime ago. In the office, the phone rang. With no ward clerk to answer it, and no sign of anyone else more senior. Juliet went to see who it was. It was an outside line.

'Melrose Ward, Nurse Avery. Can I help you?' More than likely an anxious relative. But the voice on the other end sounded brittle and frightened.

'Is David — Dr Kent — is he there? I must speak to him!'

Juliet recognised the voice as that of Moira Charles, usually so cool and collected. What could have happened? Almost immediately, Juliet realised that she would have done the same, if she'd felt desperate. She'd have asked David for help.

'They're doing a ward round — Dr Whitfield ——'

'Oh, hell! I must speak to him — I've got to see him ——'

'Can I get him to come up to Rainbow, Nurse Charles, as soon as he's finished?' asked Juliet. At the same moment she remembered it was an outside line.

'I'm not on Rainbow, I'm at Cheltenham General. My mother — they think she's — oh, just get him for me! It's urgent!' There were distinct signs of hysteria developing. Juliet laid down the receiver and hurried into the ward.

The team had reached the pancreatitis patient and were closeted behind the curtains. Juliet drew one back slightly, looking for David.

'What is it?' asked Sister in a low voice.

'It's for Dr Kent.' David left the bedside, following her into the ward. She told him what Moira Charles had said, and his face changed. Without speaking, he walked briskly into the office. Juliet stayed outside, but couldn't help overhearing some of his responses.

'Calm down, Moira. Remember what happened last time. You can't go to pieces. Think of all you've worked for. Yes, I do understand, but I think you may be over-

reacting. Don't let me down now.' There was a long
pause as he listened, and Juliet tried to imagine his
expression. Full of concern, compassion — that was certain — love? She swallowed hard.

He was speaking again. 'If the worst came to the
worst — no, don't get worked up again, she is quite
elderly, after all — you'd still have Martin. Shall I get
him to go over? He's not far from the hospital. Now
you're being foolish again. Yes, of course I love you,
Moira. We all do. Yes, I promise. I'll get to you as soon
as I can.'

The receiver was replaced. Juliet pretended to tidy a
patient's locker. She sensed he was standing behind her.

'Thank you, Nurse Avery.' That was all. He disappeared along the ward, and Juliet hurried into the utility
room. She didn't see David leave. She didn't want to
see him leave.

Lunch was over on the ward when he returned. He
looked pale and drawn, and Juliet couldn't help wondering what had happened to Moira Charles. She had
replayed in her mind what she had overheard, over and
over again, and each time she tried to ignore his words
at the end. 'Of course I love you, Moira. . . I'll get to
you as soon as I can.'

So that was that. All the rumours were true. And
she'd been right about the red roses. Well, now she
knew where she stood. David was helping her find
Elaine simply because the subject interested him, that
was all. He had kissed her because he must have seen
the invitation written on her face.

I shall have to hide my emotions better, she decided.
So she tried not to feel envious when Jill Herbert was
sent to help him with a lumbar puncture. She tried not
to imagine his sympathetic brown eyes looking into
hers, and his disarming smile when she spoke to him,
perhaps their hands touching as she passed him the
local anaesthetic —— This is no use! she admonished
herself, rubbing energetically at a stainless steel trolley.
She began to wish she were on a surgical ward, but

there was no chance of that happening within the next couple of months. She wiped away a tear that had crept unnoticed on to her cheek.

I shouldn't have let myself fall in love with him! she thought angrily.

'Go to tea, Nurse Avery,' called Sister. Relieved, Juliet left the trolley and went down to the dining-room. The sun had gone in and everywhere seemed drab and grey. It matched her mood. She took a cup of tea to one of the small alcoves by the windows, and sat looking out. She had a good view of the hospital entrance, so she started her private game of guessing what the people were.

He looks jubilant, she thought. I expect his wife's just had a baby. They look worried, got a scruffy-looking teddy bear—must be one of their children who's ill. Wonder what she's got in that holdall? Clean pyjamas for her husband? And that looks like——

'You look lonely.'

Her heart thudded at the voice, and she wondered fleetingly if she was dreaming. Then David slid into the seat next to her, and added his cup of tea to hers.

'Just my tea break.' Juliet couldn't look at him. She stirred her tea listlessly.

'And mine. I saw you disappear in this direction, and decided it was now or never.'

'What do you mean?'

'Is something wrong, Juliet? You seem to have been avoiding me since lunch.'

'You've been very busy.'

'Yes, and I wanted you to help me with the lumbar puncture. Nurse Herbert is very efficient, but the woman was awfully tense, she needed someone like you, someone with the special touch. But Sister couldn't find you.'

'I'm sure my touch isn't really so special. I'm sure you succeeded in calming her down beautifully. You do it so well.' She was aware she sounded stilted and awkward, but how could she be natural? He had tampered with her emotions, when all the time——

'Something *is* wrong, Juliet! Why can't you tell me? Is it something to do with Elaine?'

Elaine? With a shock Juliet realised that her aspirations there seemed to have faded in the light of her latest discovery.

'It's nothing to do with Elaine. There's nothing wrong at all.' She finally turned to face him, determined to smile and not let him know what she'd heard.

'Is that meant to be a smile? It's more like a grimace. This is me, David. I'm not a photographer, asking you to say "cheese". What's happened?'

'How was Moira Charles?' She smiled brightly at him, trying to still the tremble of her lower lip. 'She sounded very upset on the phone, almost hysterical.'

'Are you really concerned?' He cast a shrewd eye at her. 'Or just naturally inquisitive? Of course, I've heard all the rumours, so I suppose you have too.'

'Rumours? You and Moira Charles? What rumours are those?'

He took her arm firmly and looked hard at her. 'Stop this behaviour at once! It isn't like you, Juliet, and it doesn't suit you. I didn't want to tell you about Moira——'

'Naturally.' And now her lip *was* trembling, and a tear hovered on her eyelid.

'Will you listen to me?' Then his voice softened. 'It isn't at all as you imagine. Moira Charles could never be the girl for me. She needs someone solid and dependable, with their feet on the ground, someone strong enough to take her instability, her neurotic insecurity——'

Juliet was amazed. 'This is hard to believe,' she broke in.

'It is, isn't it? Amazing how someone can appear to be so confident and clear-headed on the outside, while —— Moira is an excellent nurse, quite capable of hiding her real self when she needs to. No, I didn't want to tell you about her, because I didn't want her story to become yours. But, knowing you better now, I believe you have an inner strength she hasn't.'

He sipped his tea. Juliet waited, a little hope in her growing, after his statement that Moira was not the girl for him.

'She needs an earthier man than I,' David went on. 'I need someone ——' and he gazed into her eyes with an expression she tried hard to understand ' —someone with her feet on the ground, but capable of understanding someone who has to fly sometimes. She mustn't be afraid to fly, herself, dreaming dreams, hoping for magic ——' He stopped and took her hand.

Dreaming dreams, hoping for magic. Juliet held her breath. Oh, yes, she understood that.

'I'll tell you about Moira—in confidence, of course. She was abandoned by her mother when she was a year old, and her father gave her for adoption.'

Juliet drew in her breath. 'You mentioned someone you knew ——'

He nodded. 'Moira was in her twenties when she decided to search for her mother. I know all this because she was engaged to my brother. Martin's a vet in Cheltenham. To cut it short, she found her mother, who rejected her yet again.'

Juliet sat rigidly in her seat.

'She didn't seem to be too badly affected by this. It wasn't apparent. But, without warning, she broke off her engagement. I believe she was afraid she might be rejected by Martin. And, in time, that was what she felt had happened. She believed Martin had ended the engagement, and eventually she had a serious mental breakdown. Martin feels guilty for not preventing it, but she refuses to see him. I have acted as mediator, tried to help in her recovery.'

'And succeeded,' said Juliet softly. 'She's back at work.'

'It's not the end of the story. Recently, Moira's adoptive mother fell ill. She was eventually taken to hospital, and this morning they told Moira that her condition is very serious. Treatment is possible, even the chance of a cure, but it's still very serious. I'm afraid Moira just went to pieces. I went to see her, and I've finally persuaded her to see Martin again. He's closer to hand.'

'You looked very tired when you came back,' said Juliet. She couldn't help feeling sorry for Moira, yet she envied her her closeness to David.

'You noticed?'

'Of course I noticed. I felt concerned. Do you love her, David?' The words seemed to linger on the air. He didn't hesitate.

'Yes, I love her, she's a sweet girl and she's had a raw deal, and I have to admit, it makes one feel so good when one is needed.' Again his eyes met hers, watching her reaction.

'I suppose needing someone badly enough is a sign of weakness.'

'Whatever gave you that idea?' He moved closer to her, still keeping his gaze on her face. 'Admitting you need someone is a sign of maturity. Is there someone you need very badly?'

Juliet could hardly breathe. She gazed at him and nodded, very slowly. 'But you love Moira. Her need is greater than mine.'

'Oh, my fanciful little leprechaun, always getting the wrong idea.' He touched her lips with his finger. 'When I said I love Moira, I didn't mean it in a romantic fashion. Love and pity are closely aligned, didn't you know? She's still in love wtih Martin, and he with her. As for yours truly, yes, there is someone who I met quite recently, who probably needs me no more than I need her, someone who brings out my poetic streak, and makes me believe in the little people.'

Juliet sat and listened to him, and the warm colour rose in her cheeks as she understood what he was saying. She put out her hand and he took it.

'I didn't want your search for your mother to lead to heartbreak,' he went on, moving close and slipping his arm around her. 'Moira became obsessed with finding her mother, but she ignored the way she'd been abandoned.'

'I was abandoned,' said Juliet, in a small voice.

'Moira was left in the middle of a shopping mall, for anyone to find. Well, now you know her story, and you'll understand why I didn't want it to happen to you. I don't think I could cope with your heartbreak.'

Juliet didn't know how to answer. Was he saying he loved her? He seemed to have suggested it earlier, with his talk of the little people. He meant leprechauns. Because it was all making her feel emotional, she tried to change the subject. This was the staff dining-room, after all. She couldn't start crying in here!

'Your grandmother rang me last night. She wants me to go and see her this evening, after my shift ends.'

'Why didn't you tell me before?'

'Because she still sounded mad at me, and I thought you might try to dissuade me. But I am going, David!'

'I have no intention of dissuading you. And I shall go with you. How else would you get there?'

'I was going to cycle——'

'Rain is forecast. And high winds.' He grinned at her. 'Even the weather's on my side.' Juliet didn't answer, but snuggled against him, not caring if they were seen. 'This is very nice,' he murmured. 'But don't you think it's time you got back to the ward?'

Juliet looked at her watch and shrieked, leaping up. 'Oh, gosh! Sister wants me to do Donna's Hickman catheter.'

'I'll walk with you, I'm going up to Folliott—the asthma patient.'

'I heard about him. How you saved his life.'

'Rubbish!' He laughed, linking his arm in hers, and they left the dining-room. When they finally parted company he gave her a kiss on the cheek. 'I'll pick you up at your house at quarter to six. Look after Donna for me.'

Juliet chatted to Donna as she flushed out the catheter. The girl was a bit depressed because neither of her brothers matched her bone marrow.

'You never know,' Juliet joked, to cheer her up, 'I might match. I've been specially tissue-typed.'

'For me? Oh, Juliet, you are a love! You will come and see me when I'm discharged?'

'Haven't I already promised? We were born on the same day, in the same place. We must have something in common!'

'Yes, I find that intriguing,' said Donna. Juliet had told her a little about her own adoption, and her search for Elaine, but nothing about her talk to Celia and her great-aunt.

'I can't go back to college just yet,' said Donna. 'I shall still be on these drugs for some time yet. It would be great if a match could be found. Will you cross your fingers for me, Juliet?'

'I'll do more than that. I'll tell all my friends to go and get tissue-typed.' Juliet finished her task and wheeled the trolley away. She couldn't help wondering if Donna had any inkling of the reason for the mismatch with her brothers.

I'm only guessing, she reflected. It's a fantastic notion, but it would explain everything.

David arrived early. Juliet herself had not long arrived home, and was still changing into her chambray shirt-waister and high leather boots when the doorbell went. She heard her mother answer it, and their exchange of greetings. Irene called up the stairs.

'Juliet, David's here.'

'Just coming!' She dabbed some perfume on her throat and ran downstairs. David was waiting in the hall, tall and attractive in a navy blazer and grey gabardine trousers.

'Come along, leprechaun,' he called softly as she reached him, and he kissed her gently on the lips. Irene looked puzzled.

'Leprechaun?' she queried.

'Just a joke between us,' said Juliet. Irene smiled.

'I offered him a cup of tea,' she said. 'But he says you don't have time. Tewkesbury for six, he said. Something important?'

'Mrs Maybury,' Juliet reminded her. 'I don't expect I shall be late back.'

Irene gave her a wry look. 'I don't expect anything of the sort. Anyway, you've got your front door key.'

'Good heavens, Mum, I shan't be that late! We're only going to see David's grandmother.'

Irene smiled. 'Have a nice evening.' They went out to the car.

'I did think,' David began, as they moved away, 'there's a nice little restaurant just opened in Tewkesbury, not far from the Abbey — cosmopolitan sort of menu, so I've been told. Once we've seen Granny, it should still be early. What do you think?'

'It sounds nice,' said Juliet cautiously, as they crossed the Severn, en route for the A38. 'David — don't you mind my going to see her? I did upset her on Sunday.'

'Yes, you really put your foot in it, didn't you? I didn't want to think that your suspicions might be well founded, but — well, now she wants to see you again, you must have been right. Of course, she may be seeing you to tell you she's suing you for slander.' He pulled a comical face.

'David! But honestly, why do you think she's changed her mind? What do you think might have done it?'

'Perhaps she's been thinking things out and she feels a bit sorry for you.'

'I hope not. She didn't sound sorry on the phone. Quite the opposite.'

'My grandmother finds it difficult to show her true feelings,' said David. 'I think it's a family trait. We hide our hearts, you might say.'

Juliet was silent. There seemed to be a danger in hidden hearts, she felt. How many opportunities, how many loving relationships had been lost because of masked feelings? Perhaps Moira and Martin had almost lost each other because they were afraid to let themselves go. Yet if I say I love him, she thought, watching his capable hands on the wheel, I may frighten him away. I must go slowly, persuade him to reveal his own heart.

'What are you thinking?' he asked. They had reached Tewkesbury.

'About you. And Moira. And Martin.' Time for honesty.

'Remember what I told you. And here we are.' He drew up outside. A white Mini was parked at the kerb. Juliet wondered whose it was.

She rang the bell, and the dog barked. This time, when the door was opened, a small black and white spaniel ran towards them, jumping around excitedly, and only stopping to sniff at Juliet's ankles. Mrs Maybury sent him inside. She seemed surprised to see David again.

'There was no need, David,' she said. He kissed her on her lined cheek.

'I know, but it wasn't the weather for cycling.' He grinned at Juliet. 'And it was an excuse for an evening out.'

'I see. Well, you're family, so it doesn't really matter. Come on in.'

Celia Hazell was there, seated on the sofa. She got up. 'I'm sorry about this, Juliet. I'm afraid it's my fault——'

'Nonsense!' said Kate Maybury sharply. 'Let's talk first, then I'll make us a drink. We may need something stronger than tea after what I'm going to tell you.'

Celia moved to an easy-chair, so that David and Juliet could sit together on the sofa. The dog trotted up to make a fuss of David.

'Lie down, Patch,' said Mrs Maybury, sitting in her high-backed chair, facing them. 'Are we ready?'

Juliet couldn't understand why she felt so nervous. She wanted to giggle; she had expected them to be told to hold hands and summon up the spirits of the dead.

'The reason we are all here,' Kate Maybury began, 'is because Celia rang me yesterday in a bit of a state. Your questions on Monday, Juliet, about Lilian Parsons had bothered her.'

Juliet had sensed this, but was still puzzled. It didn't quite fit in with her theory.

'She also told me that Jamie and Gary were found to be unsuitable as bone-marrow donors for Donna. She'd almost expected this, and I asked her why. And it was then she finally asked me a question that has bothered her for twenty years. It wasn't just the blood-groups that worried her; they merely confirmed her suspicion. And she thought Alan might suspect the wrong thing.'

'But surely, Granny,' put in David, 'that is nothing to do with us. It's Celia and Alan's problem.'

'It is everyone's problem. Donna's, mine, Alan's — and yours, Juliet.'

'Mine?' Juliet's throat was dry.

'I'll explain. It all began forty-four years ago. Celia will be sure to remember. She was nine years old and my daughter Mary was six. Despite the difference in their ages, they played well together. One day they went further than they intended, were playing by a pool, when Mary fell in. She would have drowned, but Celia saved her life, she jumped in and pulled her out, even though she was out of her depth. It was witnessed by a number of people, so I know it's true. Celia saved Mary, and Celia couldn't swim. Celia, bless her, made light of it, said it wasn't deep. Can you imagine how I felt? My only child — I'd been advised to have no more — and Celia saved her life. There was nothing I wouldn't do for Celia. Nothing!'

'Oh, Auntie!' Celia protested. 'Anyone would have done the same.' Juliet and David looked at each other. Juliet had realised that if Mary had drowned David wouldn't be sitting there next to her. Perhaps he had had the same thought, because as their eyes met something seemed to pass between them, some spark of longing they both recognised.

Kate Maybury went on, 'The girls grew up. Mary married young and settled down. Celia became a teacher, and married later. She became pregnant. She was thirty-three when the baby was born. I happened to be on duty at Thorn House while she was there. It was a long and painful labour, and it broke my heart that I could do little to help her. I was the only midwife

that evening, waiting for a relief to arrive. I rang the
doctor, hoping he would suggest transferring her to
Tewkesbury or Evesham, but he was out on a coronary
emergency, so I had to wait. Believe me, if I could have
used forceps, I would!'

She spoke vehemently. And Juliet's theory was growing into a distinct possibility. She could feel her stomach
churning with excitement.

'What about Lilian Parsons, Mrs Maybury?' She had
to know if she was right!

'I'm coming to that. Believe me, Juliet, I didn't want
to tell you this, but if I hadn't I know Celia would, and
she doesn't know the true facts.'

'You can't blame yourself, Auntie,' Celia said quickly.

'Of course I blame myself. There's no one else to
blame.' Mrs Maybury spoke curtly. She looked at Juliet.
'While I waited for the doctor, worried stiff, a girl
arrived, advanced in labour. She wasn't booked at
Thorn House, told me she was five weeks early. At first
I didn't believe her. She was working at the old people's
home, just up the road——'

Juliet shot a glance at David. Did he remember?
They'd looked at it on Sunday.

'And one of the care assistants brought her in—a girl
from the village, Shirley something-or-other. I couldn't
send the girl anywhere else, she was too near to delivery.
Her name was Lilian Parsons, she was twenty,
unmarried. I soon discovered she had her dates right
and she was premature. And there was a good reason
for the prematurity.'

'Twins,' breathed Juliet. David took her hand and
squeezed it.

'Twins,' repeated Mrs Maybury. 'She didn't know it
was twins. For some reason she hadn't seen a doctor for
some months.'

'She talked to me,' Celia put in eagerly. 'Most of the
other mothers looked down on her because she was
single. But I liked her. From what she said, the twins'
father had deserted her once he knew she was pregnant.
She told some of the other mothers he'd died, but she

wasn't a good liar, and she gave them different reasons for his death. She hadn't planned her story at all.'

Juliet sat as if turned to stone. 'Why didn't you tell me all this on Monday?' she asked Celia. Her voice sounded brittle.

'I couldn't. I liked her — I suppose in a way I felt indebted to her, but I wasn't certain. And I felt sorry for her because she'd lost — one of her —— It died.'

Celia stared at the carpet, her face flushed.

Mrs Maybury ignored her niece's interruption and carried on. 'I was still waiting for the doctor to arrive. I was very worried about Celia's baby. She delivered before he came. And at the same time, Lilian was coming up to the second stage. I'm afraid I was more concerned about Celia — the baby's heart rate had become very erratic.'

'Understandable,' murmured David.

'The baby was a boy, he was stillborn,' said Celia quietly. Juliet could feel her heart racing. David's grip on her hand tightened.

'Yes,' said Mrs Maybury, 'he was stillborn. Dead, I believe, for at least ten minutes. I rushed him away, to a little ante-room between the two delivery-rooms, knowing it was too late for resuscitation. But I tried. I didn't know what to tell Celia. She asked me about him, and I must have said it was a boy, and he was resting. How could I tell her the truth, after all she'd been through?' She looked defiantly at them. No one said anything.

'I suppose,' she went on, 'I would have had to tell her it was dead, eventually. I was trying to put off the evil moment. It was Celia, after all, who had saved my child's life!' She paused, breathing hard. 'Lilian delivered easily, with no complications. The first baby, a girl, was a good size, and lusty. The second one — well, I almost hoped it would be a little shocked, as they often are, because of the idea that had suddenly come to me.'

The atmosphere in the room was tense. David gave Juliet an encouraging smile.

'The second twin didn't cry straight away. Before it

could, I cut the cord and took it into the ante-room. Then it cried. It was another girl. I was a little disappointed, but I could only hope that Celia was still a bit hazy from the drugs. I went back and told Lilian the second twin, a boy, had died because the cord was round its neck. She accepted it.'

'You gave the second twin to Celia?' demanded David. 'How could you, Granny?'

Mrs Maybury turned to him. 'Wouldn't you have done the same? This was the girl who'd saved your mother's life. Lilian, a girl who had acted irresponsibly, didn't really want a baby at all. What would you——?'

'You can't say that!' Juliet burst out. 'She did want me! I know she did!' David put his arm around her.

'But she had two!' argued Mrs Maybury. 'Celia had none, and had suffered more. I owed Celia everything — she shouldn't have suspected——' Her voice seemed to falter.

'I did, Auntie,' said Celia. 'Now you know I did. I remembered your saying it was a boy. I said so, and you fobbed me off with the excuse that you'd been talking about Lilian's twin. But they hadn't been born then.'

'Why didn't you tell someone?' asked Juliet.

'Would you? I'd got a baby — forty-two hours in labour, but I'd finally got a baby. Of course I suspected where it had come from. Lilian had had two, and now she had one. Of course I felt guilty — I'm as guilty as my aunt. But I felt I wasn't harming anyone. Alan has never known — at least, I don't think he knows. I shall have to tell him now. For twenty years I've wondered whether my suspicions were well founded. The blood-groups confirmed them. But I didn't want anyone thinking I had been unfaithful to Alan.'

'Did Elaine never suspect anything, Mrs Maybury?' asked Juliet.

'I'm sure she didn't. But why do you keep calling her Elaine? Her name was Lilian. And I think it's fruitless going on about blame and suspicion and guilt. What's done is done. It can't be changed.'

'How can you say that, Mrs Maybury?' Juliet was astounded. 'You did Celia a favour — she deserved it, I suppose, but you parted me from my twin sister without a single qualm. Did you think it didn't matter?'

'You'd never have known, if it hadn't been for the tissue-typing,' Celia pointed out.

'You mean you'd never have told me.' Juliet tried to keep the anger out of her voice. 'All right, you never thought it necessary to tell me, but what about Donna? You — both of you — must have know that a twin sister could be the saving of her life! Didn't you ever consider Donna? Or were you more concerned with giving the impression that your lives had been spotless, untarnished? Was that more important than Donna's life?'

She felt David's hand on her arm, heard him gently hushing her. Red spots burned in Kate Maybury's cheeks. Juliet waited for the furious words, just as it had happened before. She turned to David.

'I'm sorry, David, I've said too much——'

'No.' Mrs Maybury's voice was decisive. 'You are quite right, Juliet. But I hadn't considered the implications of a twin sister on Donna's illness. But think of this: if you hadn't turned up, asking questions, we wouldn't have found you, would we? So the issue wouldn't have arisen.'

'That's true,' David agreed quietly.

'I was going to tell Donna,' Celia said suddenly, her voice trembling a little. She glanced at Juliet. 'I was going to discuss it first with Juliet. Now I shan't have to.'

Juliet and David exchanged glances. Mrs Maybury slumped in her chair.

Celia went on. 'I'd guessed Donna had a twin sister — somewhere — and I — oh, I know this sounds silly, but I've been thinking about it, ever since the transplant was mentioned, before Juliet made me realise who she ws. And I thought of putting something in the paper, asking anyone born on April the tenth that year at Thorn House to get in touch. I knew there could only be one person.' She stared round at them, defiantly. 'They do it on radio, too, and it works!'

'Yes — well —' Mrs Maybury's voice was gruff. 'So you're braver than I am. Well, I should have realised. You always were the brave one.' She sounded weary and old. For a moment Juliet almost felt sorry for her.

'Juliet —' David spoke earnestly, 'I know it seems like a disaster to you at the moment, but look at it this way. You've got a twin sister now, even though you haven't yet found your mother.'

Juliet was finding it almost impossible to absorb. Her theory had been proved, yet it still seemed like a fairy story. She had a sister. Donna was her sister. She'd have to say it to herself over and over again.

She shook her head. 'I find it hard to believe. I always felt an affinity with Donna, I thought it was because we were born the same day —'

'You're not identical twins,' said Mrs Maybury, getting to her feet, 'but I saw the resemblance straight away. I hope one day you'll forgive me, Juliet. I did think I was doing it for the best. Perhaps it was selfish of me, I so badly wanted to put a live baby into Celia's arms —' Her mouth quivered slightly and she turned away. 'I'll make us some tea.' She spoke flatly.

Celia got up and followed her into the kitchen, and there were muffled sounds of crying.

Juliet and David sat and looked at each other. He kissed her lips softly, gazing into her turquoise eyes, still dark with feeling.

'Lost a buck and found a dollar,' he murmured.

CHAPTER TWELVE

THE small restaurant in Tewkesbury was called the Menagerie. It was got up to resemble a jungle, with prints of animals and birds on the walls, mosquito netting draped around, all in shades of khaki and saffron. They were shown to a small table in the corner, next to a life-sized plaster wolf.

As David ordered, Juliet sat and looked at him. She felt she could gaze at him for ever. It was while she was sampling her genuine Spanish paella that she remembered something Mrs Maybury had said. She paused, her fork halfway to her mouth, and stared at David.

'Is something wrong with it?' he asked. 'This gammon is delicious.'

'Your grandmother said ——' Juliet began.

'I thought we'd decided not to have a post-mortem.'

'It isn't. But she said Lilian had been working at the old people's home just down the road. We saw it, David! Don't you remember? Chestnut House, it was called.'

'I remember. But it's twenty years ——'

'The girl named Shirley was from the village. People in the village will know her, even if she's left. She might have stayed at the home for years—people do. Oh, David, it won't do any harm to try!'

'You want to go to Birkleigh now? It's nearly half-past eight.'

'I could telephone, ask about Shirley. What a pity we don't know her other name.'

'I suppose I shall get no peace until you do.' He smiled tolerantly at her. 'You and your detective work.'

'My detective work has found me a sister, David. Not a mother yet, but a sister. Wait until I tell them at home! I bet my mother can't wait to meet Donna!' Juliet's eyes shone with happiness. David watched her.

179

'Did anyone tell you you were the most enchanting leprechaun ever?'

'If I'm a leprechaun, then so is Donna!'

'So she is. No wonder she's always been my favourite cousin. Eat up, and we'll go and phone.'

A senior care assistant was in charge of Chestnut House when they rang. She had a Welsh accent and said her name was Glynis. When Juliet asked about staff who had been there twenty years ago, she went into a long rigmarole about the different jobs she'd had, and her family problems, then digressed to the present staff. Finally Juliet managed to get a word in edgeways.

'I'm looking for someone named Shirley who was a care assistant at Chestnut House twenty years ago,' she explained.

'We've got a Sandra—do you mean her? She's been here a long time, about ten years. Perhaps you'd better talk to our Matron, Miss Vinall. She's been here a long time, on and off, she knows the place well. She'll be on duty tomorrow.'

'Can I come in the morning?' asked Juliet, as David nodded.

'Of course. I'll tell her. Amery, did you say?'

'Avery—Juliet Avery.'

'All right. Oh, I've just remembered, her name's Shirley.' Glynis put down the phone.

'The Matron's name is Shirley!' Juliet turned to David with excited eyes. 'Do you think——?'

'Probably coincidence. Do you fancy a walk by the river?'

'It's getting dark.'

'Where's your spirit of adventure? It's too early to go home.' He took her arm and she nestled against him as they walked back to the car.

'I want tonight to last forever,' she murmured. 'Perhaps that's silly, because tomorrow I may find out something important. What I really wish is that every evening could be like tonight. I feel so happy I could cry!'

'Please don't. Crying females always make feel guilty.'

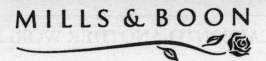

MILLS & BOON

ESCAPE INTO ANOTHER WORLD...

...With Temptation Dreamscape Romances

Two worlds collide in 3 very special Temptation titles, guaranteed to sweep you to the very edge of reality.

The timeless mysteries of reincarnation, telepathy and earthbound spirits clash with the modern lives and passions of ordinary men and women.

Available November 1993   Price £5.55

MILLS & BOON

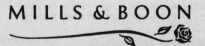

'I want to hug and kiss everyone!'

'Will I do for a start?'

'Why not?' She moved into his embrace, putting her arms around his neck, drawing his face down to hers. She felt heady with excitement, and her skin tingled. His mouth found hers, and she parted her lips in response. His arms held her tightly to him as if never wanting to let go. He murmured small endearments as he kissed her neck and nuzzled her ears. Then he gently released her.

'I think that will do for starters,' he murmured huskily. 'Come on, let's go down to the river.'

Tense with anticipation, Juliet climbed into the car beside him. He didn't speak as he started the car. She watched his hands on the wheel, wanting them touching her, stroking her skin, caressing her body and making it come alive. She studied his profile in the dim light, his firm jaw and sensitive mouth, his brown eyes that could freeze in anger and burn with emotion, those incredible eyelashes; in that moment she knew what love was, knew she wanted to spend the rest of her life with him.

Love and joy seemed to explode inside her, threatening to spill over into cries of happiness. She held it within her, afraid to breathe, relishing these moments as she sat near him, almost touching.

David was very quiet. As they drove down Lower Lodge Lane to the Severn, he glanced at her once, noticing her set expression, obviously feeling her tenseness. They reached the river, and got out.

It was still warm, and very quiet; all the day's picnickers had long gone home. David put his arm around Juliet and they walked across the grass to the riverside. A moth flew past her face, making her jump, and his grasp tightened around her waist. Birds and animals were settling for the night; a nightjar churred, a mallard made a last leisurely circle near the riverbank and then disappeared, a moorhen called 'cock-cock-cock' to no one in particular.

'This must be what the Garden of Eden was like,' Juliet said in a hushed voice.

'Are you going to offer me an apple?' asked David.

A shiver ran through her. The sky was darkening
rapidly. A long way away a cloud of sand martins
wheeled in the air before roosting.

'Shall we sit here?' asked David gently, and laid his
jacket on the grass. Too tense to speak, Juliet sat beside
him. He sat and looked at her.

'Sweet little leprechaun,' he murmured. Juliet held
her breath. Could she tell him she loved him? Was this
the moment? She turned to look at him, and he drew
her gently down on to the cool grass.

He slowly drew her to him, and their lips met. As
night fell over the river, the only sounds to be heard
were cries of ecstasy and long sighs of surrender and
fulfilment.

Juliet lay in his arms, her eyes closed. David's breathing was soft and regular. She opened her eyes, and, as if
sensing this, he turned towards her and kissed her soft
white neck.

'Don't you think we ought to get back?' he asked
sleepily.

'I'd like to stay here all night, watch the stars come
out, and the sun come up, and know that the air that
touches your skin touches mine too.'

'Romance must be catching.' He gently tweaked her
nose. 'And you'd probably get pneumonia. And then
I'd have to look after you.'

'I'd like nothing better. I love you, David.'

'There must be a response to that. Give me time and
I'll think of it. Come along now.'

They sat in the car for a moment. Juliet was full of a
warm glow. It made her want to call to everybody: I'm
in love! I'm in love! David reached out to start the car.
Then he stopped and turned to her.

'I've thought of the response,' he said, lifting her chin
with his finger. 'I adore you, especially your eyes like a
kingfisher's wing, I cherish you, I worship you, idolise
you, live only for you, treasure you.' He gazed into her
eyes. 'Oh, I forgot — I love you. Will that do?'

She gave a little nod, unable to speak. He kissed her.

'I'm so happy I could burst,' she whispered.

'At least you're not crying.'

'I never imagined it would end like this. Just a short time ago I was no one in particular, then I wasn't even that, with no one, no roots. The end of my world. And now—now I have Donna, and I have you!' Her voice broke.

'I think Donna ought to know, don't you?'

'I hope she's not disappointed with me. It's a shock to find you're a stranger in your family, a cuckoo in the nest. I hope she'll like me.'

'Who could fail to love you?' Her heart swelled.

Later, as she pulled the sheets around her and listened to the night sounds from her bedroom Juliet rememberd the birds on the river, and the cool grass beneath them, and the love they'd shared. Sighing, she fell asleep.

Next morning, at breakfast, Juliet told Irene what she'd discovered.

'So I haven't got any leads on Elaine yet—she *is* Lilian, as I thought, but I have found a twin sister—Donna. I'm sure you'll love her, Mum.'

'A twin sister? That's amazing. Oh, it takes a bit of getting used to.'

'It does. But isn't it fantastic? I've always wanted a sister!'

'Yes, I know you have. It hurt me as much as you.'

Juliet hugged her. 'It won't make any difference if I do find Elaine. You will always be my only mother. And Dad, of course.'

'Drink your coffee, or you won't be ready when David comes.'

'Do you like him, Mum?'

'Well, I haven't seen much of him yet, but I do like what I've seen. He seems sincere and he looks kind. I'm a little bit suspicious of charming men, you know.'

Juliet smiled, remembering Nigel. 'I'm in love with David.'

'That's wonderful, darling! Does he feel the same?'

'I think so.'

'Are you getting engaged?' It was obvious Irene could already hear wedding bells, and the patter of little feet.

'It's a bit soon ——'

'Yes, of course it is — you hardly know him. I'll tell your father tonight, since you won't be here. About Donna, of course, not the other.'

Excited, Irene spread another slice of toast, when she usually had only one.

'I shall tell Donna about us today,' said Juliet. 'I don't know how she's going to take it.'

'I suppose one can understand how Mrs Maybury felt, and the position she was in,' said Irene. 'I might have done the same myself, in her place. I mean, Elaine *was* so young, and so unready for motherhood.'

Juliet was silent. She would try to understand Mrs Maybury's motives. Perhaps once she had a child of her own, David's child —— But it wouldn't be easy.

David came early, ringing the bell eagerly, as if he could hardly wait. Juliet had put on a white cotton dress with black spots, and a scarlet jacket in case it rained. David showed his admiration with his expression.

'What happened to the twelve-year-old?' he said, kissing her.

'The twelve-year-old has grown up,' she reminded him, blushing slightly.

'You don't need to remind me. Are you ready? I've done a swap of shifts with Terry Baines. I shall have to work all day tomorrow.'

'I'll come and help you.'

'I wish you could, darling. I'd planned on taking you to Malvern to meet my family, but, it'll have to be another day. Soon, because I want to show you off, my little leprechaun.'

'I shall be back for lunch!' Juliet called back to her mother, and they went down the path to the car.

Juliet was beginning to feel a sort of affinity for Birkleigh. It was a pleasant, unspoilt village, yet not too far from main towns.

'I wouldn't mind living here. When we're married,' she told David, observing his reaction.

'A little cottage with roses round the door, a tabby cat on the wall, and a babe in arms?'

'Sounds divine.'

He laughed. 'I think we're a couple of romantics at heart.'

They stopped outside Chestnut House. Looked at more closely, it needed a lot of renovation. Juliet rang the bell, and it echoed in the hall. A plump, dark-haired woman answered it, and when Juliet said who she was, she beamed at them.

'Come in, come in. I'm Glynis. I told Miss Vinall you'd be coming. This way.'

She ushered them into a small cluttered room where a middle-aged woman in a navy dress sat behind a littered desk.

'Sit down,' she said cheerfully. 'I'm trying to make order out of this chaos, but it's a losing battle.' She laughed. 'I'm Shirley Vinall. How can I help you?'

When Juliet mentioned Elaine Webb she frowned and looked puzzled. 'Are you sure? The name sounds familiar — I've read it somewhere, and the Webb bit.'

'Lilian Parsons, perhaps?'

Her face lit up. 'Lilian? Oh, yes, I know Lilian well.'

'*Know* her? You have contact with her?' Juliet couldn't believe her luck. David looked anxious.

'Only by letter, dear. She's in America. She's been there for — oh, it must be twenty years. We've always kept in touch, ever since she worked here. She left to have a baby——' Miss Vinall stopped and stared at Juliet. 'Of course!' You do look like her! You're the baby she had adopted! Oh, she'll be so thrilled! She always hoped you'd try to find her.'

Juliet could hardly contain herself. David was smiling at her happiness. 'She made it very difficult,' he said.

'How did you know she worked here?' asked Miss Vinall. Juliet explained how it had all started, then she found she was telling her about Mrs Maybury and Celia. And Donna. Miss Vinall's eyes widened.

'She had twins? She never told me. Just a girl, she said. She'd had her adopted. I was just a care assistant

then, and I didn't know her too well at that time. But I
suppose she had no one else, so we started writing. I
feel I know her like a sister now — she's younger than I
am — but she never told me about the twins. I'm not
surprised.'

'That she never told you?' asked David.

'No — that it was twins. She was huge! Went into
labour early. The matron we had then, a supercilious
woman, told me to take her along to Thorn House, as
they'd know what to do. I went to see her, a couple of
days after the baby was born. And it was about a week
later she came to see me. No baby. It had been adopted,
she said. She cried. Heartbroken.'

'Then why did she give me away?' asked Juliet.

'She'd been offered a job in America, nanny to a
widower with two small children. She married him. She
often said in her letters, if only she'd known how it was
going to turn out, she'd have taken the baby with her.
But he had stipulated a single girl, and she'd assumed
he wouldn't want children. It broke her heart.'

Juliet sniffed. 'I might have been American.'

'And I wouldn't have met you,' added David.

'I can see you're both very much in love,' said Shirley
Vinall sentimentally. 'I nearly married once, but he let
me down. I went away to do nursing, and then I came
back here. I like the old people, they're my babies.' Her
thin face softened. 'I felt so sorry for Lilian. She was
badly let down by a married man — Irish, I think.' Juliet
caught David's eye. 'He didn't tell her about his wife
and children until she was pregnant. Webb, his name
was, Malcolm Webb.'

'Webb!' breathed Juliet. 'That makes sense. What
about the Elaine?'

'I think she had a sister called Elaine. No idea where
she is.'

'Didn't the police come and see you when I was
abandoned.'

'How could they? They were looking for Elaine
Webb — that must be where I read the name. I vaguely
recall the event, but I didn't take much notice. I mean,

Lilian had had her baby adopted. And I believed her.'
Miss Vinall smiled at Juliet. 'And now you've turned
up. And you've got a twin sister. I suppose you'll want
to write to Lily?'

'If she wants me to.' David squeezed her hand.

'I'm sure she does. Look — here's her address. She's
in Maryland. I know the address by heart, I've written
so often. She's got a son.' Miss Vinall wrote on the back
of an old envelope. 'I do wish I were more organised.
But as long as the old folk are happy, that's all that
matters. This is a very happy house.'

Her eyes crinkled when she talked about the residents,
and Juliet decided she liked her. She took the envelope
and pushed it into her bag. They stood up to go.

'I'm so glad it was you she met twenty years ago,'
said Juliet, as she shook Shirley's hand. Glynis chatted
as she escorted them out. As they went down the drive,
Juliet reflected that the flaking paintwork didn't really
matter. What mattered was the kind hearts that were
inside.

They sat in the car, and Juliet looked at the scribbled
address on the envelope. Maryland, USA.

'My other mother,' she whispered. 'One day.' David
smiled, and they drove away from Chestnut House.

Juliet wondered what Irene's reaction would be when
she told her she had Lilian's address. She needn't have
worried.

'So you've found her. I'm so glad.' There were tears
in her eyes as she hugged her.

'Yes, I've found Lilian. Not my mother.'

'You'll meet her one day,' said Irene, and handed
round the custard creams. David said nothing.

When Juliet reported for duty, she was sent to check
on a new patient with a severe heart infection — bacterial
endocarditis.

'She had a tooth extracted last week,' said Staff, 'and
that's how the bug got in. Rheumatic fever as a child,
so the infection settled there, on the weakest spot. She's
on complete bed rest, antibiotics, plenty of fluids. She's

had an ECG and blood tests. TLC is what she needs now — tender loving care.'

It reminded Juliet of David. The new patient didn't need anything, so she went in to see Donna.

'Home tomorrow,' said Donna joyfully, 'at long last! I can't wait for my hair to start growing back again.'

'What's the point?' joked Juliet, feeling a sudden closeness to the girl. 'Baldness is in fashion. And anyway, if you need a transplant you'll lose it all again.'

'Too true,' agreed Donna morosely, and they both laughed.

'Donna, I have something to tell you. It's very important.'

Donna grew serious. They sat on the bed together. 'It's to do with the blood-groups, isn't it?'

'Well, yes. Who told you about the blood-groups?'

'No one. I saw the tissue-typing results when Dr Whitfield came round yesterday. He put them on my table, and I read them upside down. I already knew mine was different from my mother's. Juliet, it's different from all the family. My father isn't my father, is he?'

'It's not quite —— '

'I tried to ask Mum about it, but she changed the subject. Doesn't she think I'm old enough to know the truth?' Donna sounded angry and tearful.

Juliet took her hand. 'She probably didn't want to upset you, just before you go home. Besides, it isn't as simple as that. It's a long story.'

Donna stared at her. 'Why have you come to tell me? Why not David, or my mother?'

'Because it involves me too.' Quietly, Juliet told the story from the beginning, just as Mrs Maybury had done. Donna listened with an expression of dawning horror. When Juliet had finished there was silence. Donna looked up, incredulity written across her face.

'I don't believe it. My great-aunt exchanged me — for my mother's dead baby? It's too fantastic to be true! It has to be a joke!' She grabbed Juliet's hand. 'Is it a joke?'

Juliet shook her head. 'I felt like you at first, then I

realised what it meant. I had a twin sister I might never have known about. More than that, a twin sister I had already begun to love dearly, called Donna.'

The two girls looked at each other, as if they were searching for the similarities. Tears started to trickle down Donna's face and Juliet had to swallow hard. She dared not cry on duty. Then they fell into each other's arms.

Behind them, the door opened quietly. 'I'm sorry, I'll go away again——'

Juliet whirled round. 'David!' He came and sat on the bed with them. He carried a piece of paper.

Donna smiled shakily and blew her nose. She glanced meaningfully at the linked hands of Juliet and David. 'I wondered when you two would get around to it,' she joked. Juliet went pink.

'I've got your tissue-typing result, Juliet,' said David, and laid it on the bed-table. They looked at it, and Juliet's eyes widened.

'A perfect match! I just knew it would be!'

'It almost had to be, didn't it?' said Donna.

'Do you think everything's going to turn out all right, David?' asked Juliet.

'As far as I'm concerned, everything has turned out all right. My favourite cousin is in remission, a transplant is now possible, my favourite girl has found her natural mother — and I have found the girl I want to spend the rest of my life with.'

He took Juliet in his arms and kissed her. Donna was crying again.

'Don't mind me, I'm just so happy!' she wailed. 'I always cry when I'm happy. You go away and get married or something.'

They looked at each other and laughed. Hand in hand, they left the room. Outside, Juliet lifted her face to David's. 'I feel like crying, too,' she whispered. 'Most of my dreams have come true.'

'One day we'll visit America,' murmured David, holding her close. 'One day.' And he gave her the kiss she was waiting for.